NIGHT OF THE VAMPIRE

BLOOD MOON SERIES
BOOK 3

TERRY SPEAR

PUBLISHED BY:

Wilde Ink Publishing

Night of the Vampire

Copyright © 2024 by Terry Spear

Cover Copyright by Terry Spear

All rights reserved. No part of this book may be reproduced or transmitted in any form or by any means, electronic or mechanical, including photocopying, recording, or by any information storage and retrieval system, without written permission from the author, except for the inclusion of brief quotations in a review.

Discover more about Terry Spear at:

http://www.terryspear.com/

Print ISBN: 978-1-63311-097-7

Ebook ISBN: 978-1-63311-096-0

Karen Hackett, thanks so much for loving my YA Blood Moon series, and looking forward to the next one in the series. This one is dedicated to you!

PREFACE

Night of the Vampire Synopsis

Arman dreams of a teen he met two years earlier when he realizes she's in trouble. Even though he stays with his Welsh prince vampire friends through thick and thin, this time he's certain he has to rescue her on his own. They're not about to let him though. As friends since the Black Death, they stick together. Besides, they're already known as rogue vampires who help humans and hunters in need, so what else is new? But this time the teen is a huntress, though she doesn't know it. She's held hostage by a powerful family of vampires, also that she's clueless about, and they want her for her dream abilities when she turns eighteen during the red blood moon.

Fiona doesn't like living with her eccentric great aunt who gives her no freedom until the night of the Halloween dance, big mistake on her great aunt's part. Fiona meets the teen of her dreams, she thinks, and the same guy she'd run into two years earlier in Dallas, Texas. But how could he be in Portland, Oregon now? Where she is? At her high school dance? She's drawn to him like she has never been to anyone else, but before long, he whisks her away into a world she has never known—of vampires and hunters. Of witches and dream powers. Of danger and deceit. Somehow, he must keep her safe while she harnesses her abilities to do the same for him before the blood moon makes its appearance and it's too late.

PROLOGUE

Two Years Earlier, Dallas, Texas

RARELY DID Fiona Wilder's brother take her to the mall. But she was sixteen and didn't have her driver's license yet and to her surprise Justin had agreed to drive her. At eighteen, he was already in college, and she couldn't wait to go too.

"So how are Mom and Dad?" Justin asked as they walked through the mall. He was six feet tall, dark-haired, and dark eyed, nothing like Fiona. He was studious and wanted to be a doctor.

"Dad's drunk after work as usual and Mom stays out of his way as much as possible. Well, me too. But the fights about money and his drinking go on. And you know Dad. If she hides his bottles or pours his whiskey into the kitchen sink, he goes to the pub or just gets more at the liquor store." Fiona was surprised her brother was sticking close to her. She thought he would just drop her off at the mall and do his own thing, then they could meet up and he'd leave her at the house afterwards.

"What about you?" Justin glanced down at her, and she saw the concern in his dark eyes.

She shrugged. "I have two more years to live there before I can escape our dysfunctional parents. You got through it. I'll get through it also." She adored him for caring. And for protecting their mother from their father during his drunken outbursts when Justin had still been living at home.

"You can't stay with me at the dorm," he said.

"I know."

Justin ran his hands through his dark hair. "I wish you could."

"I wish so too."

"We don't have any other relatives except for Uncle Nat and Aunt Bea, but we've never even met them. I couldn't locate them to see if you could live with them or with someone else possibly." Justin sounded apologetic.

Fiona appreciated that her brother had attempted to find another place for her to live. She hadn't known he'd tried. "I've asked Mom about that too. She said that they are on the move all the time. She said she thought they were with the CIA."

"You don't believe that, do you?" Justin asked, sounding incredulous.

"No. Who knows what they do to make money. Maybe it's illegal."

"I hope not. Our grandparents are all gone," Justin said.

"We don't know about Dad's side of the family. We could never ask him about them, or he would go ballistic." Which she thought was odd, but they didn't even know if he had brothers or sisters, who his parents were or anything. So that was a dead end.

"Right. If...if Dad ever gets violent with you or Mom, call 911 and then call me."

"I will." Fiona was surprised that Justin seemed so worried for her. He had been so glad to leave home and go away to college that she thought he hadn't really cared about what was going on at home any longer. She certainly didn't blame him for not even coming home once he got away from there. Once she left, she was never going back.

They went to the food court, and both got sodas. "I'm checking out the phone shop. Do you want to go to any shops and then meet up with me back here to have lunch?"

"Yeah, sure." She smiled, glad her brother had brought her to the mall. This had been the first time she had seen him since he moved away three months ago. She knew he'd been keeping up with schoolwork and making lots of new friends while still enjoying the company of his pals from high school. Keeping in touch with his high school sister hadn't been a priority.

He waved at her and headed for the phone store. She turned to walk to a nearby clothing store and ran smack dab into the cutest guy she'd seen in forever, spilling her dark, sticky soda all over his black T-shirt, jeans, and sneakers.

"Ohmigod, I am so sorry!" She couldn't believe the mess she'd made all over him. Immediately, she expected him to blow up at her like her dad would have if she had done that to him.

But the dark-haired teen actually smiled at her, his eyes sparkling with good humor. "No problem," he said. "I'm Arman. And you are?"

"Fiona. And I...I can't believe I did that to you. I'm so sorry."

Three male teens were standing next to him, all smiling also. The redhead of the bunch said, "He should have apologized to you for running into you."

Ha! *She* was the one who had turned so quickly and walked right into tall, dark, and gorgeous. But the redhead had sounded dead serious. She hadn't looked where she was going. Arman had just been there and was now wearing her icy soda.

"Why don't I buy you another soda to make up for it?" Arman said.

"Oh, no."

"Can I buy you lunch?" Arman persisted.

"Uh, thanks, but no. I'm so sorry." Fiona was so embarrassed her cheeks had to be brilliant red. She said she was sorry one last time, and hurried over to a trash can, threw out her empty soda cup, and went into the clothing store, wanting to disappear, thinking what a catastrophe that had been!

ARMAN and his friends watched as the girl tore off.

"She was cute," Ruric said.

"She's human." Arman headed for the men's room. His friends followed him. "You could wait for me outside the men's room."

Levka said, "We're going to, unless you need help or direction."

Arman shook his head. Levka often led their little band of princely vampires.

"Not me," Stasio said. "I'll go get you a new shirt."

"Thanks." In the meantime, Arman took off his shirt in the restroom, planning just to rinse it out and dry it under a dryer if Stasio couldn't find anything in a hurry. But Stasio used the vampire way to move—disappearing and reappearing before Arman had even finished washing the soda out of his shirt. At least his pants and shoes only had a little bit of the soda splashed on them.

"Here," Stasio said. "It's not black, but it was the best I could do on such short notice."

"Did you appear in front of anyone?" Arman asked him, eyeing the pastel pink shirt. "Pink? Really?"

Stasio smiled, then was serious. "No one saw me. I was careful. I appeared behind a rack of clothes. And then I grabbed the first shirt I could find."

Arman tossed the sticky soda-covered one away and pulled the new shirt over his head. "You know as long as we live…" He quickly washed away the soda splatter off his pants and shoes.

"Yeah, yeah, karma, and all that." Stasio laughed and they headed out of the men's room.

Ruric and Levka smiled.

"Looking good," Ruric said.

They watched as Fiona came out of the shop with a package and saw her glance in their direction, her eyes widening when she saw Arman had changed into a pink shirt. She smiled. Arman smiled at her.

But then some guy joined her. An older teen. He was carrying a package from the phone store and led her to the food court.

"Do you think it's a boyfriend?" Stasio asked.

"Brother," Ruric said.

"Why do you think they're related?" Arman asked Ruric. "They don't look like they were at all." Not as dark-haired and eyed as the young man was, and as fair as Fiona was.

"I heard her talking to him about spilling a drink on a guy and her brother said that he'd never known his sister to be that clumsy. Was it on purpose? Then she poked at him with her package in a humorous way."

Arman had seen her poke at him. He didn't know why, but he felt drawn to her. There was just something that…well, he couldn't pinpoint what intrigued him so much about her.

Stasio slapped him on the back. "She's not one of our kind."

Levka smiled. "Come on. Let's grab some lunch, but not at

the food court, and then we'll get what we need and head out of here."

"To the vampire club tonight in the warehouse district?" Ruric asked.

"Yeah. To the club tonight," Levka said. "But we don't want to get into any trouble this time."

Arman hoped Levka hadn't just jinxed them.

1

Two years later, Scotland

ARMAN RETIRED to bed early at the elder vampire's estate in Scotland, well, now it was his and his friends' estate after putting the elder vampire down who had owned it. After the big battle to overthrow the League of Vampires, Arman had started having dreams of Fiona. She was the beautiful blond-haired girl with bright green eyes of seventeen who would be eighteen soon that he had met at the Dallas mall. She'd been visiting him in his dreams for weeks now, though she was a human, not a vampire like him. He'd wondered if it was because he'd met her at the Dallas mall when she'd spilled the soda on him. Yet he hadn't been having dreams about the accident.

He'd wanted to have lunch with her. Dinner even. He had been totally smitten with her. Something about her just appealed—her apology, embarrassment, the sweet but guilty smile she had shared with him. Even though he was a vampire, he'd felt in that moment, she had...mesmerized him like the gaze of a vampire could.

He'd just wanted her to know that he wasn't upset with her in the least. But she'd shyly declined and hurried off to join an older teen, her brother, if Ruric had been right about what he'd overheard. Not that Arman had been all that surprised. Arman had been a stranger, and she probably hadn't trusted him. For good reason. Sure, he was a good vampire, but if she knew what he really was, she would have probably thought he was a monster.

Even when Arman saw her in his dreams, she was so real, so wonderful to be with that when he woke, he felt she would be there, sharing a smile with him, a kiss, a hug.

But this time when Arman drifted off to sleep, he felt tension, anxiety, concern and knew right away something was gravely wrong.

A blond-haired man came to him in his dreams, his eyes an intensely soulful green eye, and said, "You have to go to Portland, Oregon and save the girl in your dreams. She's cursed with a gift and vampires who are evil to the core want that gift. Regina Peckinpah and Tobias Farrington, to top the list. They have taken her hostage, though she doesn't know it. I beseech you to take her to safety and protect her until after the night of the blood moon when she turns eighteen."

"What's the girl's name?"

"Fiona Wilder. You've met her before. In Dallas. It wasn't a chance meeting," the man said.

"Who are you?"

"Someone who has a keen interest in her welfare. I need you to do this. You feel the connection between the two of you. You have to do it."

"What do you mean we didn't meet by chance?" Arman asked.

"Everything happens for a reason."

"Fate?" Arman didn't believe in fate.

"You need to take her to your safe house. Don't delay or it will be too late."

"By...?" Arman needed a timeline. If he believed this, he had to still fly out and that would take time.

"Before the blood moon." And then the man faded away and was gone.

It was nighttime, darkness cloaking everything, but Fiona was there in the darkness, listening to whispered voices, alarmed, unable to learn what was going on.

Arman immediately thought of the blond-haired man who had warned him to move her out of the harmful situation she was in. He wanted to talk to her, to ask her what was wrong in the worst way, but he could never speak with her. She couldn't speak to him either. It was just enough to be near her. But he worried that the man who warned him to save her was right and Arman had to do something about it—and pronto.

They were separated this time though. Seeing her through a bedroom window of a house he didn't recognize, he tried to get her attention. Somehow, he knew he had to get her out of there. He didn't know why. But he feared she was in trouble. If he got her out of the house, would she recognize him? Would she go to him willingly? Would she leave with him without a fight?

She went outside to see what the scratching noise was on her bedroom window. It was Arman, trying to reach out to her without waking the vampires in the house.

Before Arman could go to her, someone went outside to join her. He saw glimpses of a woman, powerful vampire—a rogue—Regina. Crap. Fiona wasn't a vampire. At least he didn't think she was. Unless vampires telepathically communicated, or they showed off their elongated canines, they couldn't tell if someone was a vampire or human. Or Fiona could even be a hunter, who were just as powerful as vampires, but didn't have the need for blood or the teeth that would extend. But she wouldn't be living with the rogue vampires then.

Fiona went back inside. He had to whisk her away to somewhere safe. Someplace like the estate he was living at now in Scotland.

Then he saw her in a different place. She was wearing a martial arts uniform, all white, cinched with a black belt. All around her, dead people her age with ghoulish faces and blood-splattered clothes were dancing. It was at night, music playing in the background, and Fiona was standing off to the side, looking like she didn't want to be there. He could feel her sense of not belonging, of wanting to escape. He felt an urgency that he hadn't ever felt before. He had to go to her, reach out, remove her from there, save her before it was too late. The blood moon was coming. Fiona was turning eighteen then. He had to save her before then. It could be a matter of life or death.

He had a hold of her hand. He was drawing her out of the place, the wild music still playing, but a fight had broken out between a mummy and a guy wearing a toga. "Come with me," Arman pleaded with her. "Come now."

But she broke away from him. She released his hand, unwilling to leave with him. It was dangerous to stay behind. He had to come up with another plan. A plan that would remove her from the rogue vampires' grasp.

A door slammed shut in the distance, muffled voices speaking in another room, waking Arman. He realized it was morning, but he couldn't let go of the dream he'd had. He wrote it all down, but he couldn't quit thinking about it. He had to save her. He knew it with every fiber of his being.

Wanting to do what was right, Arman walked into the living area where he heard the other Welsh princes talking. He had to tell his friends he was leaving for the States. Though he was usually the one who didn't take risks and didn't want to upset the League of Vampires, he always stuck it out with them. Levka, Ruric, Stasio, and Arman had been friends since the Black Death had turned them into vampires. Over the centuries, they'd helped humans in need—to the league's consternation.

The ruling vampires felt humans needed to take care of themselves. This time, he had to go it alone and he didn't want to tell his friends why he had to leave. They would think he was crazy and would try to stop him.

"Here comes Sleeping Beauty," Ruric joked. "We already had breakfast. Do you want some tea?"

But Stasio was frowning at Arman and looked a little worried. Maybe because Arman felt so agitated and Stasio sensed it.

Likewise, Levka furrowed his brow. "What's wrong?"

Arman didn't take a seat with his friends and ran his hands through his hair. "I've...I've got to go to Portland, Oregon."

"What?" Ruric wasn't joking about anything now.

"I need to be gone for a while and I need to do it alone." Arman knew they wouldn't go for it as soon as the words left his mouth.

Levka folded his arms. "What exactly are you saying, Arman? You know we always stick together. We watch each other's backs. We're safe here. Jasmine has her assassin job here and is taking down murderous rogues. Caitlin's learning new witch's skills every day. We've overthrown the League of Vampire's old guard and we're doing well for a change. Why would you want to go to Oregon?"

"Where *are* Caitlin and Jasmine?" Arman asked, surprised they weren't there.

"Caitlin is buying more ingredients for her potions in the city and Jasmine is trying to track down a rogue vampire that she needed to eliminate. Jasmine left a couple of hours ago. Even though Stasio wanted to go with her, he isn't in the assassin's guild and besides, she prefers going it alone," Levka said.

Arman was surprised Levka hadn't gone with Caitlin. Even though she could manage on her own now, he still worried about her overly much.

Unable to come up with a really good reason that Arman had to go alone, he shrugged. "Sometimes we need to take a break from each other."

Stasio shook his head. "When we fought the Marcher Lords, you were on hiatus that time, too. And we had to rescue you from the earl of Chester's wrath when he caught you with his daughter."

"A duke had torn the girl's gown. It wasn't me who did such a thing. How many times do I have to remind you of that? Just because I heard the girl screaming and showed up to aid her, the earl of Chester thought for certain it was me who had been the culprit. The girl was too scared to speak out against the duke who had done the deed since her father owed allegiance to him."

"Yeah, well, the duke wouldn't have gotten away if *we* had been with you," Stasio said.

"That was centuries ago," Arman reminded him, knowing that Stasio would use yet another history lesson to deter him from leaving them behind.

Ruric cleared his throat, and everyone glanced at him. He had a mop of wavy red hair that he said made him look more like his Viking ancestry, though Arman still thought he might have Celtic origins.

Arman raised his brows at Ruric who had their attention, but still didn't speak.

"What?" Arman couldn't help feeling annoyed. He had to do this, and he didn't need his friends to get involved this time. Especially if this all turned out to be dreams or nightmares and none of it was real.

"I'm ready to make plane reservations, if we're all going to be flying somewhere," Ruric said, opening his laptop on the coffee table.

"This isn't about some girl, is it?" Levka's dark eyes narrowed, and he leaned forward on the chair. "You can't go back to the States. Not without us."

They heard footsteps and everyone turned to see who it was. Smiling, Caitlin entered the living room, carrying several small sacks of herbs and other items she needed for her potions. "I picked up some essential ingredients for my new online assignments and…" She paused and considered everyone's dark expressions. "What's wrong now?"

The princes were so often in trouble that it wasn't hard to presume that something was gravely the matter. *Again.*

Levka rose and joined Caitlin, giving her a searing kiss on the lips, which caused a few woots from the other guys. She deposited the bags on the floor and then he moved her to the sofa to sit with him. "Arman wants to return to the States."

Caitlin didn't say anything for a moment, then she smiled brightly. "Okay, so we go."

"Alone," Arman said, pacing. "I'm going alone." He just knew Fiona desperately needed his help, and he hadn't seen his friends in the dreams at all. That must mean he had to do this on his own. Not only that, but she seemed to really be into him. Kissing him even. All he knew was he was in love. So he thought. What if when he went to rescue her, she didn't feel the same about him? That it was all just a dream? Or that she wouldn't even be where he thought she should be? That it was just a mixed-up manifestation of having really liked her from the first time he'd seen her.

Then again, he hadn't had any dreams of her until more recently and then the blond-haired guy seemed to confirm she was in trouble. Arman still needed to learn the truth. If she was in Portland, and she needed him, he would help her no matter what happened afterward.

"What is this truly about?" Levka asked. "Ruric will make

our plane reservations, but we need to know what is going on and where we actually need to go."

Arman sat down on one of the soft plaid sofas. "Fiona Wilder needs my help."

"Fiona Wilder?" Ruric said.

"Yeah. She's in peril," Arman said. "I just keep having dreams of her and then I had one last night of a man who said I need to save her before the blood moon. That she was in trouble. He said to bring her to the safe house—"

"Fiona Wilder?" Stasio snapped his fingers. "The girl who ran into you, literally, at the Dallas mall and she dumped a cup of icy soda all over you? That was the night we had to save the teen girls in the warehouse district from some guys, but then we had to flee, right? We all knew she had intrigued you, but she was just human. But...you're having dreams of her? Like of the soda-spilling incident?"

"No. It has been different. Like current dreams. She's nearly eighteen." Arman wasn't about to tell them that he had been kissing her in his dreams. He knew they would think he was just dreaming what he wanted to see, not what was potentially going to happen. He had never had premonitions of anything before. "It started several weeks ago. I think they're dreams, but what if they're visions, premonitions of something to come? I can't stop thinking of her. But last night, a man came to me, beseeching me to save her. Then I saw her, and I tried to take her away. In the dream, I know she's in trouble. She was..."—he knew they would really think he was off his rocker—"surrounded by dead people who were dancing."

Arman swore everyone's jaws had dropped at the same time. But no one was laughing, which surprised him. "I have to help her."

"Tell us more about what happens in your visions?" Caitlin asked, completely serious.

"A vampire family has taken her prisoner. They're evil to the core. They're the worst kind of vampire scum. They're a powerful family. Regina and Tobias."

"Even I've heard of them. Why do you think you can handle this all on your own?" Ruric asked.

Stasio was on his laptop, tapping away at his keyboard.

"I could slip in more easily if all of us aren't there," Arman insisted. "And what if these are just some kind of crazy dreams I'm having and there's nothing to it? That Fiona is still in Dallas and not anywhere near Portland, Oregon? That none of what I've seen has any merit?"

Jasmine entered the living room and must have caught some of the conversation as she joined Stasio on the sofa and kissed him. "What have you seen that might not have any merit?" As an assassin, she was used to doing that and truthfully was an excellent asset to their little pack of vampires.

"Did you take down your assignment?" Levka asked.

"Yep. And I got paid for it." Jasmine slapped an envelope of cash on the table.

Ever since Jasmine had joined them, she always shared her money with them, though they were all wealthy as many centuries as they had lived and had their money in investments. So did she, but she just was generous that way with them, which was a complete change for them from when they had first met her. She'd been a lone vampire hunter, taking down the worst kind of vampires for a bounty.

"He's having nightmares about a young woman who has been taken hostage by a vampire pack," Levka told Jasmine. "Well, it sounds more like he has been having visions, premonitions of her."

"I will go with you. If they're evil vampires, it's my job to assassinate them," Jasmine said.

Arman was glad she was with them and on their side, even

though he had been worried about her initially, since they were still considered rogues in Wales and Dallas, and she took down rogue vampires.

"In your visions, do you see that you're doing this alone?" Levka asked, trying to get to the bottom of this.

"I don't see anyone else but Fiona and me and the wicked vampiress who holds sway over her. But she isn't the only one to worry about. Tobias, blackhearted devil of a vampire, is running the show."

"Who?" Jasmine sounded like she was ready to add him and the woman to her terminal list.

"Regina Peckinpah and Tobias Farrington. They're vampires through and through, turned at the time of the Black Death like us, but they're evil to the core," Arman said. "Fiona Wilder is human, as far as we know."

Levka cleared her throat, "Good. Then we're on a mission to—"

Jasmine said, "Eradicate them in—"

"Portland, Oregon," Arman said.

"I'm on it." Ruric got on his phone to make their plane reservations. "I'll get a rental home near where these people live."

"You've found their address?" Levka asked.

"You bet. Regina's anyway. It's in a really nice neighborhood bordering Forest Park. She appears to be living high on the hog," Ruric said.

So at least the part about Regina living in Portland, Oregon was true as far as Arman's dreams or visions were concerned.

Stasio was still tapping away at his computer and shook his head. "I found the information on them. Fiona's family was cursed."

Cursed? Everyone looked at Stasio for clarification.

"In the histories of vampire families, at least the really powerful ones, the Peckinpah family is one of the most controlling." Stasio was the historian of the bunch so he would know. "But Fiona isn't a vampire. She's a huntress. Supposedly, her parents died in a car accident and her brother died in a separate auto accident. Then suddenly she has these new relatives who appear out of nowhere and take her in? They move her from Dallas, Texas to Portland, Oregon."

"She's a huntress?" Arman asked, shocked. No wonder he was having so much trouble compelling her to come with him in his visions. Vampires couldn't use mind control on hunters.

"So she *is* a hostage?" Caitlin asked.

"Or the vampires convinced her they were her relatives," Stasio said.

"But she's a huntress?" Arman couldn't believe it. If she knew he was a vampire, she wouldn't have been kissing him, he didn't think. He was disappointed to be sure. Then again, a human wouldn't be happy with it either if she knew the truth. But of course, it could still be just a dream as far as the kissing part was concerned.

"And the curse?" Caitlin asked.

"That only a vampire who is good of heart can save Fiona from the curse," Stasio said.

Everyone smiled.

"So you are that vampire?" Jasmine asked Arman, sounding surprised.

"I've been having the visions." Arman knew he had to be the one.

"Tell us exactly what you see again," Caitlin said.

"It's Halloween. I'm at a party. I see her. I try to get her to go with me. But it doesn't work out. The next thing I know, I'm at the Peckinpah home and I'm trying to entice her to leave, but it doesn't work either. But I have to get her away from them. The dream is in a different order each time, one time at the party, one time at the house first."

Stasio said, "An Egyptian girl is living with Tobias. She's bad news and works with them, doing anything they ask of her. She's our age and you better believe that they'll use her to watch Fiona's every move, so no one can get to her."

"Then you'll need us to help you out." Levka appeared a bit exasperated with Arman for even thinking he could do this alone.

That was decided then. Levka often made the decisions for the group, though he did listen to everyone's suggestions, and they were not only ready to go, but everyone insisted on it.

Arman sighed. "If this is all a mistake—"

"Then we'll have had a great adventure out of it," Caitlin said, "and I've never been to Portland, so maybe we can do some things there if this turns out to be nothing at all."

"I agree with Caitlin," Jasmine said. "I don't have any cases right now. So I'm free to go and take care of these vampires."

Arman sighed. "If I don't save this girl, it's on your heads."

Levka slapped him on the back. "If you don't save her, it's because one of *us* do the deed instead. We will free her and protect her, never fear."

2

Dreaming, Fiona Wilder tossed and turned. She'd been having weird dreams, well, weirder than usual. A blond-haired man told her to get out of the house as soon as she could. That a man would come for her. A man she'd met before. But who?

"You'll know him when he comes for you. He'll be persuasive, intriguing, and have your best interests at heart. You must trust him," the blond man said to her.

"Who?"

"They've lied to you. Regina and Tobias. They've lied. They want you for their dark purposes. You have to get out of there while you can."

"Who is coming for me? What has Regina lied about? I don't know any Tobias."

No response.

"Hello? Who are you?"

Again, no response. But then she was visited again by the guy from the mall. She was two years older, but he looked the same age as before. She'd been seeing him now for some time and every time he was just as intriguing. She wanted to kiss him again. Wanted to hug him and never let go. Only in her dreams did she escape her home life, and she welcomed seeing him again. But no matter how much she wanted to speak with him, she couldn't. Just like he would look at her with his riveting gaze and wouldn't say a word.

"Arman," she wanted to say. "Take me away." If she could leave Great Aunt Regina's home for good and join her brother in Dallas where he was in college, she would be thrilled.

Arman was holding out his hand to her, willing her to go with him, bright lights flashing all around them. Where was she? Where were they?

Off in the distance, she heard a car's engine, the garage door rolling up, waking her, and she opened her eyes. She blinked. She had been having the weirdest dreams of late. She got dressed and headed into the kitchen and found a note from her great aunt.

Gone shopping for Halloween. R

Yes! Fiona loved it when her great aunt left the house and Fiona was alone. She rarely did, and the only time Fiona could really be away from her was when she went to school.

Before she went to her high school-sponsored Halloween party that night, Fiona Wilder worked on some of her social studies homework, not wanting to do either. The only good thing was that her Great Aunt Regina wasn't at home right now. Fiona still couldn't believe Regina would give her permission to go to the high school for a party. Normally, once Fiona was home from school, her great aunt didn't want her to go anywhere—not even to get a part-time job, and certainly not to socialize with anyone. But Fiona had convinced her she needed the extra credit for a class. Which was true, but it was like having to accept the lesser of two evils—attending a Halloween party at her high school with people she didn't care for, or attending her great aunt's party, and that could be even worse.

Fiona was flipping through pages of her social studies book

that she was supposed to be reading, looking for the answers to the questions at the end of the chapter when she suddenly saw him again. A guy with dark brown hair and entrancing eyes that watched her intently, not speaking a word as if he were afraid to approach her. One minute, he was far away, observing her, and then the next, he was right there, dancing with her. Dancing?

He...he was wearing a black tuxedo and black shirt, and absolutely gorgeous. Where was she that he was dressed so nicely? The prom? She couldn't even tell what she was wearing. Something...white, she thought. Why would she wear something white? If she even thought of going to the prom, if she even had someone to go with to the prom, she would wear green—to match her eyes. Green was her favorite color. Even now, she was wearing a green T-shirt featuring a kitty cat with big green eyes wearing a black cape and black witch's hat and blue jeans.

But why was she having these strange visions? Since...a couple of weeks ago?

Everything would blank out when it happened and everything was strange in her visions—no background, no way to identify where she was, as if she were in a dream where the people were like scrap art—only parts of them really present, the rest a blur, blending in with nothingness.

And the dreams at night—he would come to her, speaking to her, and she would talk to him, she thought—at least of what she could recall. But this vision was so real, like she no longer saw the dining room where she was seated at the table to do her schoolwork. Then the old and very annoying grandfather clock chimed six times, breaking her out of the vision. Ugh, she had to go.

She grabbed her social studies book, notebook, and pen and ran to her bedroom. The room was decorated all in black and white, from her black comforter to the black and white photos of roses on the wall. At least the dresser and bedside tables were white so it wasn't quite as gloomy in her room as some parts of her great aunt's house. The whole place needed a makeover.

She tossed her stuff on her bed and then shut the bedroom door. Pulling her shirt over her head, she toed off her sneakers at the same time. Then she slipped out of her jeans and grabbed her martial arts karate gi from the closet. Yeah, it was a copout when it came to a costume for the Halloween party, but she hated Halloween. She yanked on her pants and then belted her top on afterwards. Black belt. She smiled. At least no one would dare to get fresh with her or give her any other kind of grief. She hoped.

Emma pulled up out front of the house in her bright red Ford Focus and Fiona hurried to pull on her white tennis shoes, then raced to the front door. But then she paused. Why could she hear her friend's car pull up in the drive? She had never been able to before, at least that she recalled.

She opened the front door, then closed and locked it. Not wanting her great aunt to show up and change her mind about Fiona going to the party, she raced to the car, yanked the door open, climbed into the passenger's seat, and slammed the door closed. "Go, Emma."

"You're worried your great aunt will stop you? You said she gave you permission to go." Emma wasn't worried they would get into trouble over it. She had a bit of the devil in her.

"Yes," Fiona said. "I mean, she gave me permission, but that doesn't mean she won't change her mind. She really didn't want me to go."

Emma had already pulled onto the road and headed for the school. "Your wish is my command."

Emma had a hot boyfriend, but he was going with some of the guys to the party and would meet her there. Fiona thought it had been weird. Why not take Emma to the party? At least Fiona was glad she didn't have to find another ride to the high school.

She probably wouldn't have been able to go then. Her great aunt wouldn't take her. She'd already said so.

Tall, blond, outgoing, and never in a fluster, Emma was everything Fiona wasn't. Well, except for the blond hair. For whatever reason, Emma had made Fiona feel welcome during her senior year, when everyone else ignored her like she was a brand-new freshman with a communicable disease. Instantly, seeing her friend, Fiona's spirits lifted some, not a whole lot, but some. Emma's blond hair was swept up in a chignon, an attempt at a period-style hairdo, while she wore a yellow southern bell gown.

Emma flashed her a chemically whitened smile, but then she frowned at Fiona's attire. "I can't believe you're wearing your martial arts uniform."

"I still can't believe your boyfriend didn't take you to the dance." Fiona knew she'd get a lecture about her choice of costume. The best defense was to go on the offense. "I thought Randy would take you."

"Yeah, if the guys ask him to go with them, he does it, forgets all about me, but when he sees me, all he'll want to do is spend the time to dance with me."

Fiona hoped that was true. She had never been to a dance at the high school here before.

When they arrived at the school, a lot of the kids were just arriving also, and headed inside the gym. Fiona had expected to see a variety of costumes from vampires to ballet dancers. What did she know?

But what did she see?

Dead cheerleaders. Dead soccer players. Dead jazz dancers.

Couldn't anyone come to Portland High School's Halloween party dressed as something less... *dead*?

Fiona and Emma went inside and immediately Emma saw her boyfriend. "Talk later." She hurried off to meet up with the guy. He was wearing his football uniform. But Fiona figured Emma would think that was cool, not something to lecture her boyfriend about. Then they were dancing.

Fiona sighed with relief. She had been afraid that maybe he was breaking up with Emma and that's why he didn't bring her to the dance.

Then Fiona's attention riveted to two ghoulish teens dancing together, a guy and a girl she knew were dating. They both gave her sickly, bloody smiles.

At seeing all the "dead" people, Fiona's stomach twisted into knotted rope. Why would anyone mimic the dead? It seemed rude, even sacrilegious. Would any of them feel that way if *their* parents had died so recently? It added another reason why she didn't like being at the party. Trying to curb her irritation, she tugged at her black martial arts belt and took another deep breath.

Rock music thundered in the gymnasium, shaking the floor and rattling the walls, while colorful rays of lights poked into the darkened room, making everything look eerily surreal. Decorated in faux cottony spider webs, jack-o'-lanterns, ghosts made out of someone's white sheets, and hideous toothy ghouls painted on poster board, the place looked bad enough. But the ghoulish students squirming on the gym floor made the most hideous scene—a vision similar to something really bizarre in some other world of an apocalyptic, zombie flick.

Reminding herself she came here to earn extra credit in social studies—a subject she definitely needed help in—she vowed to stay for one hour, no longer. The alternative was returning home to her great aunt's old people's Halloween party. She wished her parents had warned her that her Great Aunt Regina was unusual, but odd didn't begin to describe her *or* her friends. The really strange part was her parents had never even mentioned her before and then when they died she came to take

Fiona home with her and had said she was Fiona's dad's aunt on his mother's side.

Like any other Halloween, this appeared to be one more disastrous venture.

Fiona saw Emma finish a dance with Randy. He kissed her, then took off in another direction. Emma got a drink at the refreshments table, and she headed back through the twisting, turning dancers toward Fiona like an arrow shot from a bow, her drink held up high so no one would knock it out of her hand. Emma glided toward her in the yellow satin gown, the top cut low, and her breasts pushed up, looking as though she would fall right out of the gown if she leaned over just a tad. Emma smiled at her.

Fiona mirrored Emma's smile, though she couldn't stir up any enthusiasm for tonight's activities. As soon as Emma reached her, she said, "You and Randy didn't dance very long. Doesn't he want to dance?"

"He had to run to the little boy's room," Emma explained to her. "We're going to dance once he returns."

Fiona motioned to the others on the dance floor. "I'm glad we're wearing something original, and aren't one of the undead, only—"

"We stick out," Emma said, lifting the cup of punch to her lips. She always seemed comfortable with the way she was, no matter the time or place. "Besides, wearing your ju-jitsu gi isn't exactly original." Giving Fiona one of her lopsided grins, she tucked a golden curl behind her ear. She tsked in a way that meant Fiona was her social project, and somehow, she would change her into a woman of confidence. "Next time we'll do it right."

Fiona folded her arms and raised her brows. "There won't be a next time. We'll have graduated by then. The truth is I would settle for good grades in school, getting through the rest of the year living with my eccentric great aunt, and leaving all this behind. I can barely wait to live in a dorm at the university where my older brother is now enrolled in Dallas."

Emma's eyes widened just a bit, then she quickly recovered. "You haven't told your great aunt yet, have you?"

"No. There never seems to be any time to mention it." The truth was Fiona feared her great aunt might object. There was no sense in making a scene when she was stuck living with her for the rest of the school year—seven more months, but who was counting?

"Don't you think she might want you close by since you're her only living relative? Maybe to go to the University of Portland?" Emma planned to go there, so Fiona was certain that's why she wanted her to attend the same university.

But Fiona hadn't seen her brother in eons, and she wanted to be close to him, like she'd been before their parents died. "Nah, she wasn't close to my family when they were alive, so I don't know what difference it would make now."

Emma didn't respond, just tugged at one of the tails of Fiona's belt. "Showing off your black belt can only help to intimidate the guys, you know."

Fiona sighed deeply. "I don't have a date. I really didn't plan on coming, except I needed the extra credit."

"You *could* make a "c." It's not all that bad a grade." Emma was smart, but she often didn't apply herself. Her grades reflected it, but her actress mom didn't seem to care.

Fiona shook her head. "You know, even when I work really hard to earn good grades, sometimes that's not enough. If nothing else, my parents had instilled in me the importance of earning good grades in high school, especially when I plan to go to college."

"No fun," Emma teased.

"I guess I just have to wait until I go to college."

"Then you'll be busy trying to make good grades in college."

"My mom would die if I made a..." Fiona said the words before she thought, and then she felt like the incredible shrinking teen with a heartache the size of Texas, her eyes filling with tears. She silently threatened them *not to* leak down her cheeks. She gritted her teeth. She didn't think she would ever come to grips with the fact her parents were dead.

Emma patted Fiona's shoulder ineffectually, seeing her discomfort but at a loss as to what to say.

Wanting to change the subject, Fiona said, "I didn't have time to think about a costume." Which wasn't quite the truth. Deep in the recesses of her mind, Fiona had hoped Halloween would somehow just magically disappear, and she wouldn't have to think about it. She'd never felt comfortable with Halloween, All Hallows Eve, as if something dark inside her stirred. More now than ever. The dreams, the nightmares, the visions... "Besides, you're lucky you could wear your mother's Little Theater gown."

Emma nodded. "I am, but I could have dug through Mom's costume wardrobe and found something for you too."

"Right, her witch's costume from *Hansel and Gretel*."

"She has others. A sexy, fringed dress from the flapper era show she did, *Thoroughly Modern Millie*. I told you that you didn't need a date. Lots of kids come to these things, mingle, and end up going steady."

"Yeah, easy for you to say. Here comes the star quarterback." Fiona hadn't meant her words to come out sounding so... *irritated*, but now that Randy would whisk Emma away, Fiona definitely felt like a small spider hiding in the crack of a wall.

Blond like Emma, only Randy's eyes were a sapphire blue and hers more of an aqua blue, the two seemed to have eyes only for each other in the crowded gym.

Emma's smile returned. "Hmm, hey, Randy. I didn't have a chance to tell you that I love your football costume."

He smiled back at her and kissed her cheek. "I love your Cinderella dress."

Fiona was about to tell him Emma was a southern belle, but Emma said, "I'll be anything you want me to be."

Fiona rolled her eyes.

Twirling around, Emma showed off her gown. The bodice dipped enough to entice the guys, but not too low to get her kicked out of school, unless she leaned over. The skirt billowed out and reached her ankles. She looked like a blond version of Scarlet O'Hara from *Gone with the Wind*.

Emma winked at Fiona, took Randy's arm, and moved with him to the dance floor.

Fiona watched her friend dance with the quarterback hunk, wishing she could be so lucky. Though she imagined wearing her combat ready martial arts uniform probably turned any guy off, if he thought of getting fresh with her.

Then she snorted under her breath. *Right*. Guys dancing with dead cheerleaders instead was a real turn on.

Then a glimmer of light caught her eye from across the room. A sparkling lure in a crowded bowl of squirming, faux, half-rotted humans. Her gaze shifted from the shimmering ruby in the gold ring the wearer wore to see a guy dressed in a black tux, wearing a black shirt even. He was dressed to kill. She looked up at his face. He had soft, wavy, coffee-colored hair and dark eyes that studied her, not anyone else, but her. His mouth turned up instantly when he caught her eye. Omigod, he...he looked like the guy from her dreams. The guy from the mall incident. Literally. *Arman?* It couldn't be.

Just as suddenly, her whole body grew sweaty as it would when she worked out in a vigorous ju-jitsu lesson.

Now, *he* was fab. No white paste smeared on his face to simulate the undead. No streaks of red blood to suggest the ghoulish look others wore tonight.

She'd never seen him at the school before. Not that that would be unusual. As big as the Portland High School was, she could attend it forever, and never meet all the students. Heck, she wouldn't need to, once she had met one as intriguing as Tux was.

"Hey, want to dance?" A guy wearing a toga leaned against her, his words slightly slurred. His meaty hand clutched her shoulder, and his hot breath reeked of whiskey. She knew the smell well because she'd smelled it on her father often enough. The guy's grimy size-twelve sneakers nearly stepped on her size six and a half's.

Had he mixed alcohol with the punch? Or had he brought the liquor to the party in a flask? *Idiot*. The image of a younger version of her father acting like that flitted across her brain. No way did she want to have anything to do with some teen getting an early start on the same path to destruction.

Before she could shove his hand from her shoulder, the ruby ring bearer wearing the black tux appeared beside her. She didn't have time to wonder how he'd moved across the gigantic floor through all of the squirming, writhing bodies so quickly. Unless he'd already been on his way to see her. She hoped he would step in to rescue her before she had to create a scene and knock toga guy on his butt herself.

"The lady wishes to dance with me," Tux eloquently said, his hand outstretched, palm upturned, as if he was an actor in some old-time movie.

She glanced down at her gi. How could she dance with anyone who looked so suave when she looked like she was ready to do martial arts combat? And in sneakers?

The drunken kid stumbled off. "Whatever," he mumbled under his breath.

Tux still held his hand out to her, waiting for her to accept. His eyes focused on hers, willing her to go along with him.

Still, she hesitated. Guys never asked her to dance. What was wrong with this one? Didn't he know she wasn't popular? That she wasn't an adorable cheerleader with all the cute moves...that *her* moves could be deadly?

He smiled a little. Immediately, he disarmed her.

"Sure, why not? You must be new to the school." She took his hand and her whole body heated. She didn't want to call him Arman and for him not to be the same guy she'd spilled her drink on at the mall in Dallas. How odd would that be that he would be in Portland, Oregon and at her school function now?

He didn't say anything, though his eyes devoured her as if she was a tasty sweet treat that he couldn't get enough of. His attention both bothered and intrigued her. She'd never met any guy who acted so interested in her, but the notion kept darting through her mind, *why*? Why had he targeted her, when there were lots of other girls who were cuter and much more outgoing? Never mind that they looked hideous with fake blood dribbling down their faces and throats. Without all that fake gore, they were attractive. And why did he look so much like the guy in her dreams?

"My name is Fiona Wilder."

The smile returned to his lips, his eyes darkening to midnight.

"But the name can be misleading," she rattled on like she always did when someone made her nervous.

Her skin grew clammy, and she was sure her deodorant would fail her when he still didn't respond. She took a deep breath, tried to stifle the urge to keep talking about nothing at all, and waited for him to tell her his name, but still, he said nothing. Just moved her across the floor to the slower paced waltz as if he'd danced all his life. The feel of his heated hands on her body, seared her to the core. She hated what a neophyte she was when it came to being with a guy. But Bradley Stapleton had given her every reason for staying clear of the general male population last year. Which was one of the reasons Halloween didn't appeal. And because of him, she was glad she wasn't attending high school in Dallas any longer.

"Hmm, you sure dance well," she murmured, almost forgetting she was swaying to the music in clunky tennis shoes.

Thankfully, her older brother had taught her how to dance, or else she would never have been able to move a step. With tall, dark, and handsome leading her across the floor, she felt as though she'd been dancing with him for eons.

When the music ended, he still held her hand while his other rested on her hip. She smiled, embarrassed, her cheeks growing hot. "The dance has ended."

A couple of girls giggled at her as if she and Tux were the weirdest kids in school. Or maybe they were wishing they had a chance to dance with him instead.

The music began again, a faster paced number. Only he didn't let go, but instead glanced at the band members, his look dark and foreboding. Suddenly, the band cut the music, and began playing another slow dance. Tux smiled, the expression softening his hard, angular features, and he moved with Fiona across the floor. She glanced back at the band and all the members were watching Tux as if he had made them change their minds about the dance routine and would clue them in concerning the next dance scheduled.

Which was ridiculous to consider, but she couldn't help it.

She caught a glimpse of Emma watching her, her mouth agape, and her blue eyes as wide as the lake near her great aunt's home. A new flush of heat rushed across Fiona's skin. Yeah, Emma couldn't believe that Fiona would be dancing with a hunk any more than *she* could.

"Your friend?" Tux asked, his voice deeply sensual.

What was there about the guy that melted her insides into molten lava? "Yeah, my best friend."

He nodded, but she couldn't read his expression this time.

Then the horrifying thought crossed her mind—he was interested in her because she was Emma's friend? Instantly, she stiffened. If he thought that he could get friendly with her so he could make the moves on her girlfriend next...

Sure, *that* was it. He figured Fiona could offer to introduce him to her. Except Emma was glued to Randy Quarterback and Tux needed an in...being that he was probably not really into the physical stuff. First, she had the bad luck to get involved with Bradley Stapleton, who had been playing the field, unbeknownst to her, and now Tux...

She shook her head. Better to end her fantasies before they got any more interesting *and* unattainable.

"Do you want to meet her?" Fiona's voice sounded a bit on edge, though she had meant to sound sweet and innocent, not in the least bit annoyed. She wanted to growl. No wonder the cutest guy she'd seen in forever wanted to dance with her.

He shook his head, his gaze shifting back to her. He sure wasn't talkative.

"You don't want to meet her?" This time Fiona said the words so incredulously, that he cast her an elusive smile.

"No," he said, his word tinged with amusement.

A strange sense of relief washed over her. The thought the cutest guy in the school wouldn't be interested in her girlfriend, instantly set her at ease. "So you said you were new to the school?"

His dark eyes sparkled. "*No, you* said I was new to the school."

"Oh. I haven't seen you around, so I thought you might be new." She bit her lip, trying to come up with something even more brilliant to ask. She never was this tongue-tied with Emma. Why did she have to be such a klutz with Tux?

The guy in the toga approached again, and Tux's hand tightened on hers. His protectiveness, or maybe possessiveness, cheered her. She glared at the drunk. Why was it that a drunken kid was the only other guy interested in her? *Figured.*

The sheet-cloaked guy stumbled into her. "Can I dance now?"

"Sure, go right ahead." Fiona motioned to a free space on the dance floor. "There's lots of room." There wasn't much floor space for a couple, but if Toga Guy danced by himself, there would be room enough.

He laughed, but his tone wasn't amused. He grabbed her arm with the grip of a gorilla, his fingers instantly bruising her easily bruised skin.

She would have taken care of the guy effortlessly with one of her own martial arts moves, just a twist of her arm to free herself, then a knee to the groin, and—

Before she had a chance to jerk her arm free as she had learned in martial arts, Tux touched him with the palm of his hand and shoved lightly. The drunken kid fell several feet into another couple.

The toga-clad guy jolted a six-foot tall mummy, who immediately slammed his huge fist into Toga Guy's face and knocked him on his butt.

"Fight! Fight!" several of the students chanted, like a bunch of bloodthirsty ghouls.

"Time to leave." Tux's voice was determined, brooking no argument. He grabbed Fiona's hand, then hurried her toward the exit.

"Wait! I came with Emma!" Fiona struggled to extract her hand from his, her heart thundering. She didn't know anything about the guy. Not even his name—she realized—if he was new to school or not...well, anything. What if he didn't even belong to the school? He certainly didn't act like any of the immature guys she'd met. He seemed sophisticated, well beyond his years, for being only seventeen or so. Maybe he was eighteen, or maybe he had been held back a year and was nineteen.

"Emma won't mind," he said, his tone dark and mysterious. With Fiona still in tow, he hurried her toward the door.

"*I mind!*" She twisted her arm toward herself, then down and around, freeing herself from his grasp.

"Fiona!" Emma hollered from somewhere in the cluster of students, who were vying for a better view of the fight, while two parent chaperones were racing to stop it.

Fiona turned.

"Fiona!" Emma ran toward her. "You're not leaving, are you?"

Fiona shook her head. "Not without you."

"Where's the totally hot guy?"

Turning, Fiona looked at the spot where he'd been standing. He'd vanished. He must have slipped out through the exit, but it seemed as though he'd vanished into thin air.

"Gone," Fiona muttered under her breath, her arms prickling with unease, yet she couldn't help being irritated the way things had turned out. The first cute guy who really took an interest in her...

Oh, heck, what was the use? Concentrating on schoolwork was the most important thing she could do, then getting out of here. Next year, when she was out from under her great aunt's tyrannical rule, she would have fun.

"Who was he?" Emma asked. "I don't think I ever saw him before. Man was he cute. Randy got mad at me for gawking at the two of you dancing. I stepped on Randy's feet twice."

Fiona laughed. "Uhm, well, I didn't quite catch his name."

"What?" The disbelief in Emma's look and voice made Fiona even more conscious that she'd screwed up.

Fiona shrugged one shoulder, pretending it didn't matter. Yet, when she'd torn her hand from his grasp, she'd felt a part of her soul wrenched away. "He wasn't very talkative."

Emma tucked her hair behind her ears. "He seemed to really like you. He had eyes only for you. Why wouldn't he have told you his name?"

"Maybe he's a college student. Maybe he doesn't go to our school at all."

"Ahh, sicko. Older guy after high school girls."

Figured. Fiona took a deep breath. "He seemed a lot older than the guys our age. Really sophisticated."

"It might have been the tux. But it really looked like you were leaving with him, and I worried—"

Fiona headed for the punch bowl. "Nah, I'm more level-headed than that." In fact, that's what she figured was her problem. She never took any chances, never allowed herself to have any fun. Well, except for with Bradley Stapleton, and that had been a total disaster. Then she frowned. Despite knowing she'd never met Tux before, he really seemed...like the guy from her dreams. The guy she had *kissed* in her dreams. The guy from the mall. *Arman.*

She dipped a ladle filled with punch into a cup, then glanced at a light reflecting off something sparkling through one of the windows.

Tux—his mesmerizing eyes caught her gaze through the glass.

Her heart rate sped up, and she nearly dropped her drink.

Emma grabbed her hand. "Jeez, Fiona, you look like you saw a ghost, and you're spilling your drink all over the floor."

Fiona righted her glass and stepped back from the spill, not wanting to stain her white gi.

"Though there are enough dead people dancing around here that a ghost or two shouldn't surprise you." Setting Fiona's cup on the table, Emma grabbed a napkin to wipe up the mess. But Fiona couldn't shake the feeling that Tux was watching her, though she was too busy helping her friend clean up the spill to look at the window again. If he was observing her, did he think she was horribly clumsy?

Emma glanced at the window. "Did you see someone?"

Fiona looked up, saw only blackness beyond the glass pane, and swallowed hard. "It was just my imagination playing tricks with my mind. It had to be."

A shiver of dread and something else trickled down her spine. A part of her wished she'd taken him up on his offer...to leave with him. Another part—the common-sense side that made her do what was right—cheered her on.

So why did she want to dash out into the night and search for tall, dark, and handsome at the top of the bewitching hour, and find out what other moves he had planned with her?

3

"Earth to Fiona," Emma said as she drove Fiona home. "You've been in a daze all evening. I can't believe Randy asked you twice to dance with him, and you made him repeat his question. Twice."

Fiona imagined Randy had probably never been stood up by a girl, and certainly not twice by the same one. Especially one as unpopular as Fiona. That had to be a real ego deflator.

"Sorry. I guess I didn't sleep well enough last night. Besides, Randy was only being nice because you jabbed him in the ribs and told him to ask me."

"Nah, he was tired of me dancing on his feet."

Fiona chuckled. Emma had told her she'd known Randy since she was a preschooler and as laid back as he was, Randy never got upset with her ever. Not even when she'd accidentally spilled soda on his brand-new football uniform at the beginning of the school year. Which reminded Fiona of spilling a soda on the guy at the Dallas mall. At least Fiona wasn't the only accident-prone person. Instead, Emma had told Fiona that Randy had just smiled and given Emma a kiss. He was always giving her a kiss, come to think of it. Fiona sighed, wishing a nice guy like Randy could give her a kiss, like the guy in her dreams, except for real. "I thought you were a great dancer."

"I got distracted." Emma lifted a sculpted brow. "I still can't believe you didn't learn the new guy's name."

Fiona couldn't either. Why hadn't he just come out and told her his name? Why hadn't she just come out and asked him what it was? Maybe he wasn't that interested in her.

Sure, that's why he nearly dragged her out the door when the fight started.

Had he wanted to protect her? She snorted. Yeah, right. He might not normally be a physical kind of guy. Even though Tux had shoved Toga Kid into the mummy, he might have worried the mummy would clobber him back.

Tux really didn't look like he had the kind of build that could handle muscled mummies or other threats. Yet, his sinfully dark eyes held some kind of a hold over her that could definitely be labeled *dangerous* with a big "D."

She glanced at the rearview mirror and swore a black sports car had followed them from the dance. First down the main drag, then a side road, then another street, but then it disappeared down the next one.

She couldn't shake the feeling the car had been following them. *Paranoia*. Sleepless nights were absolutely making her paranoid.

She glanced back at the road and saw a guy standing next to the road in the dark—too close...too close to the road. The headlights of Emma's car highlighted the tall, dark-clothed figure of a teen, right before he dashed out in front of them.

"Stop, Emma!" Fiona screamed at her friend but warned her too late.

Emma slammed on the brakes, the screeching sound shattering the silence of the night.

The front bumper hit him squarely in the legs with a horrible thud. For a second, he lingered on the hood, rolled off, and disappeared before their eyes.

Fiona's heart thundered, and she barely breathed. "Ohmigod, ohmigod."

Emma stared out the windshield, not moving, not saying a word.

For a second, Fiona was worried her friend had gone into shock, but what about the guy she had just ran over? Fiona began issuing orders. "Emma, snap out of it! Turn off the ignition, set the emergency brake. Call 911."

"I...I didn't bring my cell phone."

Through clenched teeth, Fiona ground out, "Great! Neither did I." Too late to regret the fact she had left it at home. She'd been running late for the party and had left it charging on her dresser. That's what she got for being out of time as usual. Jumping out of the car, Fiona dashed in front of it. The blood rushed to her ears as she peered at the six-foot tall, dead-looking, redheaded hunk. He...he looked like the guy who had been at the Dallas mall with Arman. This was just too unreal. She didn't believe in coincidences, and she couldn't believe they would all be here in Portland, Oregon suddenly, running into her in different ways.

"He just can't be dead," Fiona whispered to Emma, touching the guy's wrist. No sign of a pulse, not even a whisper of one.

Emma crept up beside her. "Is he...he—"

"He doesn't have a pulse."

Emma tugged at her long blond hair. "Give him mouth-to-mouth."

"*You* give him mouth-to-mouth! He's dead!" Fiona touched his throat, trying to find a pulse there, just in case his wrist one wasn't working. "Jeez, Emma, we've got to take him to the hospital."

"But, they'll report this to the police."

"So?" Fiona couldn't believe Emma. She was usually pretty well-grounded. Of course, running over a guy could shake anyone. Fiona shook her head and sighed, deeply exasperated. "Help me get him into your car."

"We can't."

"What? We can't leave him out here in the middle of nowhere. That's illegal," Fiona said.

"Running over him is illegal."

Her friend had a point. Fiona motioned to his tux, which reminded her of the other guy who had disappeared at the dance. "The guy's wearing black clothes and stepped out of the woods into the car's path. He blended in with the night. You didn't have time to stop."

"I don't have my driver's license yet. I mean, when Mom returns home on Monday, she was going to take me in to get the license. I'm supposed to be driving with an adult still."

Fiona stared at her. "I thought you got your license yesterday."

"I was supposed to, but Mom had to leave too early."

"Emma! I can't believe you did this to me...to us. Help me get him into your car, now! I'll drive us to the hospital." At least Fiona had her license!

He stirred.

They both stared at the guy. In the car headlights, he appeared pale, probably due to running over him and killing him, *briefly*. His hair was slightly long and red. But his lips were as pale as his skin.

Fiona ran her fingers over his arm and felt him stir again. "Oh, oh, oh, he's coming to."

Emma frowned. "You *said* he was dead."

"Don't argue with me! He groaned and his hand moved. Help me get him into your car."

"But if he has injuries, couldn't we make them worse?"

Fiona took his hand. "He's ice cold. But you're right. We shouldn't move him." She looked up at Emma. "What am I saying? We can't stay here all night, waiting for someone to come along. Help me get him into your car."

The dead guy groaned.

Both she and Emma gasped.

"Are you all right? Where do you hurt? Can you hear me?" Fiona asked.

The guy's eyes popped open, pretty green eyes. They seemed to draw Fiona into their bottomless depth. She blinked as he stared at her, then felt his hold over her withdraw as he looked up at Emma.

"*She* hit you," Fiona said, quickly. Though she hadn't meant to sound like a five-year-old who wanted a parent to know she hadn't done the bad deed.

Emma rolled her eyes and folded her arms.

A slight smile curved the guy's lips upward at the corners when he looked back at Fiona.

Was he delirious? In shock? What was there to smile about? He was mostly dead only seconds before. Even if the car didn't break any of his bones, he would surely be in lots of pain, bruises, internal injuries even, maybe.

"I'm hungry. Do you want to go to the Burger Joint?" he asked.

His dark, deep voice made Fiona think of Tux at the dance. She'd never seen a guy in a tux, accept at the prom in Dallas last year. And now two in one night? Still, she reasoned the guy had to be half out of it. Whoever heard of a guy getting hit by a car, dying, and then wanting a burger?

"We have to get you to a hospital," Fiona said, taking his hand to help him up.

"Do we have to?" Emma squeaked. "I mean, you heard him. He has got to be fine if he's hungry."

"Emma, he was dead...I mean, unconscious." Fiona didn't want to make him feel worse than he had to be feeling about it already. "That means we need to take him to the hospital and get him checked out. He's probably in shock. If we feed him, no telling what might happen. What if he has internal injuries? The food could go someplace it shouldn't."

"I feel perfectly fine," he said, and allowed Fiona to help him up. "Really, I haven't eaten in a while. Would you mind joining me at the Burger Joint? I hate eating alone."

"See?" Emma said, tilting her chin up. Then she frowned. "Mom said I couldn't let anyone ride in the car except for you, Fiona."

"She probably said you couldn't drive the car until you got your license either."

Emma frowned. "Alright. That was if I was driving. If you're driving, it could be okay."

Fiona shook her head, but she still held onto his hand. If he was alright, why was he so terribly pale?

"Please?" the guy said.

Fiona took the keys from Emma. "Alright, but I think that you eating anything before a hospital checks you out is a horrible idea. Don't blame me if you die on us again."

"In your capable hands, I'm sure you would bring me right back to life again." He smiled at her. "My name is Ruric, by the way."

She opened the back door for him. "I'm Fiona, and this is Emma. You probably ought to lie down in the backseat until we reach town."

He moved to the passenger's front door. "If you don't mind. I might get queasy sitting in the back."

Emma shook her head. "Whatever."

Anything should have suited Emma as long as Fiona didn't take Ruric to the hospital. Still, Fiona worried he wasn't quite all right.

"Do you feel nauseated right now?" Fiona asked.

He smiled when she climbed into the driver's seat. "No. Really, I feel great."

"I don't believe it," Fiona muttered under her breath. For one thing, he had to have a terrific headache. For another, where the car smacked his body, he had to be feeling some pain.

"Dead guys don't lie, Fiona." Again, he smiled at her when she glanced at him.

Emma tried to change the subject. "So you have a strange accent, and Ruric isn't a usual name. Where are you from?"

"Wales. The name means people of victory in Romania, where some of my people were from. Though some believe I have Celtic heritage. Others say they're sure I descended from Vikings."

"Cool," Emma said.

"Were you at a dance or something?" Fiona asked, this time keeping her eyes on the road.

"Yeah, a dance."

"What were you doing out in the middle of nowhere?"

When he didn't answer, she glanced at him. Again, he smiled. "You remind me of a girl I once met. She had a sympathetic way about her. Just like you. I wouldn't be surprised if you were planning to be a nurse someday."

"Not me. I can't stand the sight of blood."

He chuckled.

When she pulled into the lighted parking lot of the Burger Joint, she realized Ruric hadn't answered her question. What had he been doing in the woods?

Though he could have easily opened Emma's door for her as

he stood closer to it, he took great strides to reach Fiona's door and opened it instead.

Maybe it was because she reminded him of his old girlfriend. Maybe it was because she hadn't run him over with the car.

"I don't want to rush you or anything, but I have to be home soon. Why were you in the woods?" Fiona asked Ruric again.

"My brother was supposed to pick me up, but he had car trouble. One of the guys I know, not very well, said he would drive me home. Except he and his buddies were drinking. I told the driver to pull over and let me out before he got us all killed. So he did…in the middle of nowhere. I saw your headlights and thought I could wave you down. I guess you couldn't see me." He tugged at his tux. Even his shirt was black. "It pays to wear white when you're trying to flag down a car at night."

"Oh," Emma said, as they stepped into an order line. "What if he dented Mom's car?"

"Jeez, Emma. You should be thankful he's alive and well."

"Of course, I am. But what if there's a dent in the car?" Emma asked, her voice on edge.

"I didn't see any," Ruric said.

"But it was so dark," Emma said.

"My night vision's very good." He winked at Fiona.

Her body warmed with embarrassment. A total charmer. Just like the other guy. As if they were…brothers. "Is your brother dark-haired, per chance? Wearing a tux tonight also?"

"He's at home, so he wouldn't be wearing a tux tonight."

As much as Fiona was afraid to pose the question, she had to know. "Were you ever in Dallas?"

Ruric's eyes widened marginally. She took that as a yes.

"At a mall in Dallas, Texas?" she ventured to ask. "About two years ago? Right about this time of year?"

Emma eyed them speculatively. "You don't know each other,

do you? I mean, that could be a good thing if you had been friends."

"Not friends. I just...met someone who looks a lot like Ruric."

"Two years ago? I don't recall," Ruric said.

Fiona wasn't sure she believed him. She wished, in a way, that he had said yes. Then she would know she wasn't just imagining things. On the other hand, if he said yes, wouldn't that be a bit worrisome?

Emma tried to pay for the meals, but Ruric wouldn't hear of it. He just smiled in his captivating way, paid for the food, then carried the tray of burgers and drinks to a booth. Emma and Fiona sat across from him.

Once he'd passed out their drinks, he said, "You both attend Portland High, don't you?"

"Yes," Fiona said, poking her straw into her soda. "How did you know?"

"The sticker is on the car's bumper."

"Oh," Emma said, her voice a moan. "Can we pleeeease talk about something other than my mother's car?"

"Really, no harm done to me or the car."

"You say you live with your brother?" Fiona asked.

"Yep. He's twenty-one, three years older than me. He can be as demanding as a mother and father combined."

"And your parents?"

"They died in Wales."

"Oh. I'm sorry."

"Don't be. I never knew them. My aunt raised us. Then when my brother turned twenty-one, he brought me here when he'd found a good job."

Fiona held up her cheeseburger to take another bite. "Doing?"

"Working with a local mortician."

Emma choked on her drink, then wrinkled her nose. "Creepy."

"There's good money in it. I might go into the business myself someday."

Fiona nodded, though the idea that anyone made a living at working with dead people didn't interest her. She fingered a french fry. "What school do you go to?"

"Eastside, but I'm transferring to Portland. The girls are much prettier there."

Fiona smiled. "I'm sure you'll break a lot of girls' hearts if you leave."

"The girls had boyfriends already. A guy with a foreign accent and a strange name didn't appeal to any of them."

"I think the name Ruric sounds great. It's a name with character."

Ruric leaned back against his seat.

Emma nodded. "And he has a cute accent, don't you think?"

Fiona's gaze met Ruric's dark eyes. "It's very—"

"Entrancing? Magnetic?" he offered. A slow smile edged upward, and his eyes seemed to smile.

Fiona quirked a brow and mirrored his expression. "Disarming."

"Ah. Well, you see, Fiona, I believed I could use my powers of persuasion on you, but you seem to have an unusually powerful way of holding your own. Which is refreshing."

Fiona wasn't sure what he was getting at. His easy-going manner, and the way he paid for their meals when Emma had run him over, certainly appealed to her. Even more than that, the way he devoured her with his gaze intrigued her, as if she was the only girl he'd ever cared about. Just like the other guy had done.

When they finished eating, Fiona drove Ruric to a two-story, colonial home. But as soon as she pulled the car curbside, a guy stalked out of the house. His down-turned mouth and knitted brow gave her the impression he ruled over Ruric worse than any parent might. The odd thing was he didn't look any older than Ruric. And he sure looked like one of the teens she'd seen with Arman at the Dallas mall, though she'd only glanced at them in passing.

"Levka," Ruric said. He motioned to Fiona. "She saved me."

Levka glared at her, then shook his head. "What do you think you're doing?"

Obviously, big brother didn't like it that Ruric was interested in her.

His dark brown eyes seemed to darken further, then he glanced at Emma as if he finally had just noticed her. She remained quiet. Fiona thought she was worried Levka might grow even angrier if he knew Emma had run over his brother with the car.

"You pissed off Arman. What were you thinking?" Then Levka stormed back to the house.

Arman?

"Don't mind my older brother. He's just watching out for me. See you at school tomorrow." Ruric turned to Emma. "Chin up. I won't tell Levka that you ran over me." He smiled, then followed Levka into the house before Fiona asked him about Arman and the Dallas mall again.

"Jeez, Levka's creepy," Emma said as Fiona drove her home.

"He doesn't look any older than Ruric, I don't think. Do you?" But if Arman was with them, they were all three at the Dallas mall, and...there was one other. Was he here too? This was all just too weird.

"I didn't think so. What's up with you tonight? Two guys in tuxes had the hots for you? If Ruric asks, are you going to go out with him?" Emma asked.

"I can't quit thinking about the other one."

"The one with no name."

"Yeah, and how much he seems like...*this one*."

Arman wanted to kill Ruric for meeting up with Fiona, when this was the job he'd taken on to save her from a bunch of ruthless vampires but Stasio held him back and wouldn't let him out the door. Levka himself was angry enough about what Ruric had pulled.

"We have been friends for how many centuries?" Arman asked Ruric as he and Levka entered the house.

"We all need to help her, Arman," Ruric said, non-plussed. "I am not after your girl, though she certainly appeals. But I couldn't control her like I had hoped. She's definitely not human. And I couldn't get her to leave Emma to drive home on her own when she isn't even supposed to be driving without a license."

Arman let out his breath in a huff. "She is *not* my girl, and she is cursed! She needs our protection."

"Our protection is correct. You can't do this on your own," Ruric said. "Do not give me your condemning look too, Levka. We all agreed we had to save Arman from his folly no matter what the cost."

"I'm enrolling in her high school," Caitlin said.

"And if you need blood?" Levka asked, raising a dark brow.

Arman knew he wasn't happy with the notion.

"I'll feed at night. I can get through the day now without any problem. She might trust me more than you guys. Besides, I do have my witch's powers. We need to convince her to go with us and neither of you guys managed to do the job right tonight."

"You haven't formally finished your training," Levka reminded her.

"I know some. So she's a huntress?" Caitlin asked Arman.

"Yes. I couldn't control her any more than Ruric could, though I tried. Why her parents wouldn't have told her what she is doesn't make any sense," Arman said. "I tried to remove her from the dance with my hypnotic suggestion. I thought it was working and then she broke free. I only know we have to free her from that family. She doesn't belong with them and I'm afraid of what they plan to do to her."

"How is she cursed?" Caitlin asked again.

Stasio said, "I'm still researching the family. I still don't know. Since you've been having dreams of her, Arman, did she seem to recognize you when you met her at the dance?"

"She did. But it was more than that. We had a real physical attraction that seems to transcend time and space. And I think she might have remembered me from seeing me at the Dallas mall," Arman said.

"Oh, about that, I'm afraid she did. She asked me if I'd been there," Ruric said. "I said not that I recalled. I was afraid she would think we followed her here and would think we were up to no good. There isn't any easy way to handle that."

Arman shook his head. He hadn't thought of the consequences of her recalling that incident two years ago.

"We don't know what her curse is, Caitlin, but I suspect she has no clue she's a huntress," Levka said. "In other words, that means she's not even trained in the art of swordsmanship to fight rogue vampires."

Jasmine smiled. As their assassin, she came in handy. "Count me in for going to high school. This could be fun."

Going to school was not Arman's idea of fun, but saving Fiona was a necessity, if the nightmares he was having was any indication. "I'll be there."

Stasio was too busy to say whether he planned to go to the school with them or not as he searched documents online.

Ruric only smiled. "I'll go, but since I believe she really thinks we were in Dallas when she was."

"Which could make her all the more wary of us," Arman said, exasperated. "What if she believes we all came here for some nefarious purpose where she is concerned?" That's what worried Arman. He *should* have come alone.

4

When Emma pulled up in front of Fiona's great aunt's two-story, colonial brick house, ten cars still sat curbside and again, Fiona couldn't help but wish that she still lived with her parents. Not that her home life had been so great in Dallas where everyone made fun of her about her father being the town drunk, and her mother, the ultimate enabler, who hid his liquor, which only catapulted him into more drinking binges.

Why her mother had gone out with him that fateful night was still a mystery. Fiona couldn't help envying her brother, Justin.

"Well, here we are," Emma said cheerfully.

Fiona realized then, she'd been staring at her great aunt's house, lost in the past. "Yeah." Except for the dim lights of candles flickering behind sheer white curtains, the house looked dark. *Ambience*, her great aunt would say.

"Are you all right?" Emma asked.

"Yeah." Not really, but Fiona definitely didn't want to tell Emma about her family. It was best to pretend they were as normal as everyone else's. Though the truth was Emma's mother was kind of a flamboyant, artistic flake, and her husband had abandoned them and then got himself killed, so maybe not everyone else's families were all that normal either.

"Call you tomorrow. But it'll be later. Randy and I are going to the Oregon Coast in the afternoon."

"Seashore," Fiona parroted, when she thought she saw something travel across her great aunt's roof like a panther moving silently, swiftly—something large, black, and...a person? Oak trees stretched their massive branches over the roof, swaying in the cool breeze, casting dancing shadows across the gray shingles.

Too vivid an imagination? Or did she now need glasses?

"Fiona, I've picked you up and dropped you off at your great aunt's house what...fifteen times in the last three months since you moved here? You always seem so happy to leave her home, and so reluctant to return. Is there something wrong?"

"No, sorry. I told you I hadn't slept well last night." Though, since Fiona had moved here, she hadn't slept well any night. She couldn't put her finger on the reason either. "Listen, have fun at the seashore. Maybe we can go there together sometime."

"Yeah, get a boyfriend and we'll make it a foursome."

Fiona's hopes were instantly dashed. "Yeah, okay. As soon as I see Tux again, I'll ask him if he wants to go."

"Tux?"

"The guy I danced with."

"Sure, great idea."

A tall, thin man, dressed entirely in black, pulled the curtain sheers aside in her great aunt's living room window and stared at Emma's car.

"Got to go." If Fiona could have sneaked into the house and avoided her great aunt's party guests, she would have. But she'd been caught.

"Night, Fiona. Oh, and please don't tell anyone I ran over a guy tonight. Okay?"

"I won't. He was fine. No one needs to know." Fiona knew if she told her great aunt about it, she would never let her ride with Emma again. Fiona climbed out of the car, wondering if the man at the window realized how rude he was, staring at her like that. But it was more than rude. Defiant, as if he wanted her to know he knew she had arrived home, and she needed to get inside. Worse, she worried he would realize she wasn't comfortable at her great aunt's house and mention it to her. Relations were already strained enough.

She'd never seen the man before, his dark hair banded in a ponytail, and his soulless dark eyes watching her while she walked to the front porch. Was he worried for her safety? Or afraid she was contemplating running away?

Which she had. But where would she go? Nowhere, and she would be worse off than before.

He turned away from the window as if he'd satisfied his need to control her will. Quashing the irritation she felt, she reached for the doorknob, but the door swung open wide, and a pretty brunette about Fiona's age, smiled back at her. Startled, she stared at the teen. What was a young person doing at her great aunt's Halloween bash?

"Hi, you must be Ms. Power's grandniece, Fiona. I'm Clarissa. Pleased to meet you." She offered her hand and Fiona stood staring at her costume, the most riveting silk and jeweled, ankle-length Egyptian dress she'd ever seen. "Like it?"

Fiona shifted her gaze to Clarissa's smiling face. "It's beautiful. It must have cost a fortune."

"Garage sale item."

"Really?" Fiona looked back at the dress. No way could anything that regal have been sold as a cast off.

"Come on in." Clarissa motioned to the house as if she lived there instead of Fiona.

Yet, when had Fiona ever felt that it was home? *Never.*

The whole place was decorated in black and white. Black leather couches, black velvet comforter-covered beds, white dressers, side tables and coffee tables. White urns decorated in black cuneiform, others displaying hieroglyphics, and some Chinese symbolism sat on tables.

Even her great aunt had a black and white personality. It was either this way or that. No shades of gray. Woe to the poor soul who attempted to argue with her.

The whole house smelled of cinnamon and vanilla, the fragrance wafting from the candles lit throughout the house.

Fiona tried to slip away unnoticed, like she usually tried to fade away in her great aunt's house. Clarissa, apparently playing the part of an Egyptian princess or queen, walked in front of her and headed for the living room.

The man Fiona had seen staring out the window caught her eye. He leaned down and spoke to her great aunt sitting on one of the black couches. She nodded, her platinum blond hair braided, hanging down to her waist, her costume, some kind of Viking dress, and her feet were clad in fur-covered boots.

Fiona wouldn't call her great aunt typical. Far from it. In great shape, she wore spandex shirts and skinny jeans like a teen. No way would she let her hair go white, and she'd had eyeliner tattooed around her eyes to simplify her afternoon makeup routine. Three facelifts, too, to remove the wrinkles, and a couple of eye jobs to remove the bags, she'd mentioned to Fiona to explain how come she looked so young. No wonder she looked like she was fifty when she was closer to eighty years old. Not only that, but she was *not* an early riser. She was an all-night party girl. Yet, she demanded Fiona stay home most nights, lecturing her that evil men prowled after young women in the evening hours. Fiona attributed her great aunt's distrust to never having raised any children of her own.

Still, the spry woman wasn't at all what Fiona had expected. She had been her father's aunt and wouldn't have anything to do with them while Fiona's father went on his drunken binges, so Regina had said. Which was nearly all the time, once he'd lost his insurance job, which was due to his earlier drunken binges.

Fiona's attention shifted to the man dressed simply in black from his shoes to his turtleneck. Was he playing the part of a cat burglar? Stiff, that's what he looked like, as if he didn't really want to participate in the costume dress up bit for Halloween.

"Come in, Fiona," her Great Aunt Regina said. "Meet your Uncle Tobias."

Uncle? A streak of panic slithered down Fiona's spine. What if this man, who appeared to be in his early forties, wanted her to live with him until she graduated from high school? Her great aunt was getting awfully old, even if she didn't look or act her age.

Fiona closed her gaping mouth.

"He's not really your uncle, dear. You really ought to learn to hide your feelings better. If he wasn't so easy to get along with, he might have been wounded by your reaction."

Another lecture. Fiona swore her great aunt gave her five a day on school nights. More on weekends.

Tobias's eyes held Fiona's hostage for a moment, as if challenging her. She couldn't fathom his role here. Yet, she suspected he wasn't going to be just a casual acquaintance. Then he turned away, as if he'd become disinterested in her, the conversation, and the party. Which reminded Fiona, where were all the partygoers?

As if on cue, the sound of car engines roaring to life forced her to go to the picture window. Like in a race, nine of the ten cars parked out front peeled down the street. Where had her great aunt's friends been all this time? Had they sneaked around the back of the house, then dashed for their cars while she was inside?

Weird. That's the way her great aunt and her friends were, too. Just plain weird.

Clarissa yawned. "I've got to go. Are you ready, Tobias?"

The two were dark-haired and eyed, yet neither looked like they were related. Clarissa had delicate, refined features. Tobias was gaunt, his bones raw and masculine.

He turned his head as if he were listening to something outside, and so did her great aunt and Clarissa. Fiona strained to hear whatever they seemed to be listening to, but only heard the blood pounding in her ears.

"It's been a pleasure as always," Tobias finally said, leaned down, and kissed Great Aunt Regina's cheek.

What was worse, her great aunt acted as though the guy had the hots for her the way she nearly swooned. *Good grief.* He had to be forty years her junior.

Clarissa smiled at them, then patted Fiona's shoulder. "We'll have to get together again sometime."

"Do you go to Portland High also?"

Clarissa glanced at Tobias as if she expected him to tell her what to say. He studied her but didn't utter a word.

"I homeschool," Clarissa said, turning to face Fiona. "Maybe next year I'll join you at Portland High."

"I'll be at college with my brother in Texas." Fiona finally said what she'd wanted to for the last three months, but no time had seemed appropriate.

"We'll have to talk about this later," Great Aunt Regina countered, her voice stern.

Instantly, Fiona went on her guard. Did her great aunt not want her to leave Oregon? It certainly sounded like it to her. But she knew her parents had left them enough money to put both her brother and her through college. Why couldn't Fiona choose the one she wanted to go to?

Fiona tried to keep her cool and said to Clarissa, "You must be a junior in high school then."

"No." Clarissa smiled. "It's the homeschool curriculum I use. I'm seventeen like you and a senior."

No one got something like that mixed up. Either she was a graduating senior, or she wasn't. Though for an instant, Fiona had hoped she'd met another girl who could be her friend. It seemed anyone who was associated with her great aunt was downright odd.

Clarissa crossed the floor and kissed Great Aunt Regina's cheek. "See you later, Ms. Peckinpah."

"Yes, dear. See you both soon."

"Night, Great Aunt Regina," Fiona said. "Tobias, Clarissa." No way would she call Tobias her uncle when he wasn't, and while they were still here, she had every intention of slipping away to the privacy of her bedroom.

"Call me, Regina, dear," her great aunt said, her voice low and hard. "I've told you repeatedly it makes me sound *old* when you call me your great aunt." She smiled, but her eyes remained cold.

"Right, Regina." Ugh, it sounded so disrespectful, and downright weird. Fiona's mother had taught her better.

When Fiona reached her room, she swore she heard whispers from the living room. Was Tobias telling her great aunt she better put a tighter leash on Fiona? For whatever reason, that's the way she felt about him. Where Clarissa seemed cheerful and sweet, he was dark and ominous. How could Clarissa like such a person?

It took all kinds, Fiona guessed.

She walked into her dull black and white bedroom and decided she had a new mission. If she had to live here for several more months, she wanted everything in blue like the vivid azure waters of the Caribbean. It was her room for the school year after all, wasn't it? Surely, her great aunt wouldn't object if she spent some of her parents' money to make the room more her own.

The front door slammed shut, and Fiona plunked herself down on the queen-sized bed. She shoved off her shoes, but the sound of something brushing against her window caught her ear. She'd heard it last night also and vowed to see if shrubs rested next to it, while the breeze stirred the branches and scraped across the pane. Of course, she only remembered to check when it was as dark as the deepest part of the Marianna Trench out there.

When it was light out this morning, she'd forgotten to check it out.

She pushed her shoes back on and walked out of her room. All the candles had been extinguished. The scent of vanilla and incense still wafted in the air, and the whole house was cloaked in darkness. Her great aunt's bedroom door was now closed, which meant she had retired to bed.

Fiona was relieved she didn't have to speak to *Regina* further tonight as she was always grilling Fiona about her grades, her friends, her life in general, and it was too late in the evening to put up with that nonsense.

She opened the patio door to the backyard and walked outside. Except for one security light in the corner of the wooded acreage and a ghostly white half-moon clinging to the black satin night, everything was immersed in darkness or shadows.

The breeze stirred the trees, inspiring them to sway in an unchoreographed dance, but she swore something crunched on the leaves clustered at their base. Yet, she couldn't see anything that might have made the sound.

An owl hooted behind her, and she whipped around, seeing no sign of the feathered fowl, but she now faced the house and her bedroom. The only thing that moved beneath her windowpane were wisps of grass that reached only a couple of inches high and caressed the red bricks near the base of the house. No shrubs sat beneath her windowsill, and the branches of a small tree perched at the corner of the house didn't reach that far.

Gooseflesh erupted down her arms, and she automatically rubbed them. What was the sound she'd heard last night, scraping softly against the glass?

"*Fiona*," she heard whispered on the breeze that sent a chill straight into the marrow of her bones.

"Fiona!" Regina snapped. "Get yourself to bed. It's not safe for you to be wandering outside alone at night." She stood on the back porch in a black robe, her shimmering hair fanned out across her shoulders. Her shadowed face scowled, but then she lifted a brow and gave her a small smile. "All Hallows Eve, you know."

5

Arman wanted in the worst way to enter Regina's house, but he couldn't. He had to get Fiona outside. But as soon as he finally did, that wicked Regina made her return inside. He wasn't leaving her though. He had to reach her and get her to listen to him. He would try to communicate with her telepathically. Though it was really rare for hunters to have that ability. They had been shocked to learn that Caitlin had the ability to listen in on others' conversations. She had never had to speak with anyone using telepathic communication until she'd learned the vampires used it to communicate with each other.

Arman couldn't leave just yet.

Levka communicated to him, *"We are all waiting to hear how it is going for you."* He sounded exasperated with Arman for not telling him what was going on all along.

"I haven't been successful. Regina is keeping tight control of Fiona."

"Then return to the house."

"I will. I'm going to try one more thing." Arman hoped it would work. If it didn't, he would call it a night and try again tomorrow when they were all at school. For now, he perched in the tree, watching her window, the lights out, the curtains closed. He was just glad Regina hadn't called for backup to see if someone was coming after Fiona.

THE ONLY THING scary about All Hallows Eve was her great aunt, Fiona decided as she returned to bed and pulled the black comforter under her chin.

Just before she drifted off to sleep, she had the worst urge to look out her window again, but she was afraid she would wake herself too much, and she would never get back to sleep.

Not moving from her bed, she stared at her window, straining to hear any sound. Nothing, this time. Her eyes slowly shut.

In the darkness, blanketed in sleep, she heard someone calling to her from far, far away. Just a voice without body, a figment of her imagination—had to be.

"Fiona, dearest, come out to me."

Where had she heard that voice before? Mesmerizing, intriguing, solicitous, deep, and dark like a fathomless pit.

"I will give you everything in my power."

Fiona turned over in her bed and hugged her pillow to her cheek. "Who...?"

"I am your sweetest dreams and your protector against your darkest nightmares. Take my hand and come away with me."

"Where? I don't understand. I don't know you. I—"

"Fly away with me. Together we will find—"

Fiona waited for the rest of his words, longing to hear his hypnotic voice, but silence ensued. "What do I call you?" She sighed under her breath and opened her eyes.

The voice was so real, she felt as though the speaker had

stood in her bedroom while talking to her. He was a conundrum, a revealer of nothing but riddles.

"Not real," she said, and closed her eyes, but then the whispers renewed. She turned her head toward the bedroom door.

The hushed voices continued. From the living room?

After slipping out of bed, she tugged a robe over her green tank top and matching pajama bottoms decorated in whimsical frogs wearing golden crowns and silly expressions on their green faces. Her watch indicated three. At this rate, she would never get any sleep.

When she opened her bedroom door, a powerful spicy incense wrapped around her. She noticed at once that Regina's bedroom door was open, and the voices continued to whisper in the living room.

A spy she was not. The only time she'd tried to overhear what her brother and mother fought about—him telling her she needed to leave their dad for all their sakes, and her mom telling him their dad needed her—Fiona had been caught eavesdropping.

Goose bumps trailed down her arms when she inched her way down the hall, the sound of her footsteps cushioned by the black carpeting.

"He must be stopped," a male voice whispered.

"She must be the one to do it," Regina said, her voice hushed.

"She's just a child." Fiona swore it was Clarissa, the Egyptian princess, speaking.

"You must tell her," the man said, only this time she believed him to be Tobias.

Her great aunt gave an abrupt laugh. "She's entirely too headstrong. She wouldn't listen to me or believe me, and we need her cooperation."

Clarissa said, "Then you will lose the chance to control her power."

"True and if that happens, she dies," Tobias whispered, and he sounded like he wouldn't regret that at all.

Fiona's heart hammered as she drew closer to the living room, where not a single light illuminated the darkness. When she reached the end of the hall, the voices abruptly stopped.

For what seemed an eternity, she stared into the darkness while she leaned against the wall, wondering what everyone was doing in there. They couldn't see her, any more than she could see them. Had she made some noise that she hadn't detected, but they'd heard?

She waited, hoping she would hear them leave before she attempted to go back to bed. Fearful that if she turned her attention from the living room, someone would come up behind her, yet, she felt something urged her to look toward the end of the hall.

With a quick look, she blinked to see Regina's bedroom door closed. She nearly had a stroke, and without waiting a moment further, she hurried back to her room.

She slipped into bed and covered herself with her comforter, the words spoken in the living room running through her mind like a broken record. None of them made any sense. If Clarissa had been speaking about Fiona, why would she call her nothing more than a child? They were both seventeen and not children anymore.

Who had to be stopped? A guy. But who? She shook her head. They weren't speaking about her. Someone else. New mission. Find out who needed saving. Not that she thought she could be any help, but maybe if they let her in on the problem, she could offer...to help. What was all this business about someone having some power. And if they lost it, she would die.

Was it some kind of political situation? She'd never heard Regina speak about politics though.

Fiona yawned and closed her eyes.

The wind grew, the scratching at her window vaguely stirred her, but she was so tired...she couldn't fully wake.

Then she finally drifted off to sleep and slipped into and out of dreams. *Suddenly a blond-haired man appeared to her and said, "You need assistance. I'm trying to get aid for you. You must go with him. Go with him, Fiona. Don't delay. He'll help you get free. He'll help you escape. You're not safe. He's...safer."*

"Escape?" she tried to say to the man. But she couldn't speak. Yet, she didn't feel he was actually speaking to her either. More like he was sharing his words in her brain, not out loud like she had first thought. His green eyes pleaded with her, and she thought he wanted to draw closer, to hug her even.

But she didn't know him, yet something seemed familiar. She couldn't figure out why. She was sure she had never met him before.

"We want you safe. We have always wanted more than anything else for you to live a full and happy life. But now you're in danger."

"Who are you?"

"Someone who cares about you more than anything else in the world."

*She felt he was speaking the truth. Who was he? He wasn't telling her anything. Why was he keeping who he was secret from her? If she was in trouble, why not tell her what the danger was? Who he was? Why did he care? But when she tried to ask him any questions, she remained mute, unable to voice a word. She tried to force out a word, struggling, screaming, until she made a squeak and...*woke herself up.

For a moment, she just lay there, trying to figure out what was going on, not wanting to go back to sleep, not wanting to return to the weird dream she'd had.

"Come out to me," a man said, the same one who had spoken

to her earlier, not the one in her dream. Someone who had the most glorious, appealing, and enthralling dark voice.

But more, she thought she'd heard it before, not now, but in real life. But when? She couldn't remember for the life of her. *"Who are you?"* she asked in her head, because like the man in her dream, this guy wasn't speaking to her out loud.

None of this could be real. Could it?

ARMAN TRIED to reach Fiona again, shocked to the core that she could actually talk to him telepathically, but he knew Tobias would return and they would make a concerted effort to find him this time and eliminate the threat to their plans. He told her his name was Arman, but she didn't say anything back. *"Fiona? I'm Arman. I'm trying to bring you to safety."*

He waited and she didn't respond. *"Fiona?"* Arman said to Levka, *"I'm returning to the house we're renting out. I was able to reach Fiona telepathically though."*

"No way. Really?" Levka asked.

"Yeah, just like Caitlin. Are you sure Fiona isn't a vampire? That would explain why we can't control her thoughts also, if we're wrong about her being a huntress," Arman said.

Stasio said, *"According to the history books, she's a huntress. But you know, they can be wrong. Or information recorded to make people believe one thing when it's all lies."*

"Oh, that's not good. I thought this was a for sure thing. She seems to be asleep. Regina is asleep. Regina and Tobias don't plan to do anything tonight. They didn't come looking for me so I suspect they don't know that I've been here," Arman said.

"Good," Levka said.

"I'm returning to the rental house." Arman hated to leave without Fiona, but he had suspected this wasn't going to be easy.

Why hadn't Ruric just grabbed her when he had the chance? The girlfriend would have been a witness. But Ruric could have just wiped her mind of seeing him and made her think Fiona had returned to her house.

When he arrived at the rental house, everyone was waiting to see him. He didn't want to talk about it any further. He was disappointed in how things had not worked out for them.

6

The next thing Fiona knew, it was Sunday, and it was already afternoon. She couldn't believe it!

Rubbing her eyes, she wondered how she had managed to sleep so late. She rolled out of bed and yanked her pajamas off, then slipped into her bra and panties, jeans, and a T-shirt, socks, and shoes. As soon as she had breakfast, er, lunch, she needed to write her social studies paper and do some, ugh, algebra.

Hurrying down the hall, she rubbed her temple, wondering if all that had happened last night had really occurred. The scent of the pungent incense still lingered in the air. Worse, she heard the same voices in the dining room. Tobias and Clarissa?

Groaning, Fiona had wanted to discuss things privately with Regina. That would be hard enough to do alone with her, but she really didn't want to discuss it with the others around.

Fiona walked into the dining room. Regina raised her brows and proceeded to dish up a plate of spaghetti. "Afternoon, Fiona." She didn't sound happy that Fiona had slept so late.

Fiona glanced at Tobias, whose dark eyes consumed her while he leaned back in the chair at the head of the table and folded his arms. His dark hair was still pulled back in a tail, making his face appear even longer, more angled, and thinner if that could be possible. Instead of a turtleneck, he now wore a black satin shirt. It reminded her of her great aunt's furniture, black and white, with the white being his pale skin. Though living under the often-overcast Oregon skies, she noticed most Oregonians didn't have tans like Texans did.

Clarissa was the exception with her golden skin, but not so much from tanning, Fiona suspected. Her nationality probably had more to do with it. As beautiful as the night before, Clarissa wore a shocking pink halter-top and matching jeans, which was way too cold for an autumn day. She set a glass of water on the black tablemat in front of Fiona and flashed her usual cheerful smile.

Her dark curls cascaded over her shoulders, down her hips in satiny swirls of thick, to-die-for hair.

"I heard voices last night," Fiona said, gauging Regina's reaction. Today, her great aunt was dressed in black denims and wore a sparkly spandex top of black and white swirls.

"Did you?" Tobias spoke, his words dark, accusatory.

Fiona faced him, surprised he would comment and not her great aunt, but his arrogance made her suspect he was used to running things. His brown eyes nearly turned to black, and she realized belatedly he waited for her answer.

"Yes, I did. I'm a *very* light sleeper. Just about anything will wake me."

"And you heard?" He sounded like he was running the Inquisition. One wrong word, and Fiona would be history.

"Weird stuff."

Fiona noticed that Clarissa's smile had faded, and her dark eyes concentrated so hard on Fiona, it made her feel the girl was trying to determine if she was lying or not.

Her great aunt took a seat opposite Tobias. "Eat and tell us what you think you heard."

Think? Did that mean the three of them were ready to denounce her ravings?

Clarissa sat down across from Fiona, but none of them were eating. She glanced at the black-tile countertop. Clean.

"We've already eaten, Fiona," Regina said. "What did you hear?"

"Nothing much, really. Do you know I sleepwalk?"

Her great aunt stared at her like she'd sprouted horns and a barbed tail.

Tobias shook his head. "She wasn't sleepwalking."

"Who were you talking about?" Fiona speared a meatball and figured if they weren't buying her sleepwalking story, she might as well start asking questions and put them on the spot instead. "I mean, the dangerous guy. Who is he?"

All three stared at her, and again she really wished she lived with her brother.

"Why were you wandering around in the backyard late last night?" Tobias asked.

Regina must have tattled on her, but it annoyed Fiona that he thought it was any of his business.

Tobias cleared his throat and asked again, "Why were you outside last night?"

"I heard a scraping noise at my window. I wanted to see if there was a shrub rubbing against it."

Tobias exchanged looks with Regina. A hint of concern flashed across their faces. "I'll be back. You know what to do."

"Tobias," Regina said.

Wasn't Clarissa going, too? Fiona wished she would. The secrets they withheld from Fiona made her feel like an outsider.

The front door closed on Tobias's departure, then Regina said, "He danced with you last night at the Halloween party."

A sip of water went down the wrong way, and Fiona coughed and sputtered.

"He's a bad influence." Regina ran her long-tapered shimmering white fingernails over the black satin tablemat.

Great. Now her great aunt would lecture her about guys too. Here Regina had never shown any interest much in Fiona before. How had Regina known about him? Was someone at school spying on her for her great aunt? Things just couldn't get any creepier.

"How did you know?"

"One of your teachers called me this morning to see that you got home safely. She said a boy followed your girlfriend's car out of the parking lot. He was kicked out of school a year ago."

Her heart fell so hard, Fiona couldn't hear it beating any longer. "Kicked out of school for what?" Wouldn't you know, some troubled teen would be interested in her.

"For stalking another girl. At first, he was really sweet and considerate. Then he became possessive and domineering. The girls' parents had to get a court order to stop him from following her everywhere. Three months after their first date, someone murdered her. Though they questioned him, they could never pin the crime on him, nor did they ever find someone else who might have killed her."

Fiona's blood chilled. "What kind of a car did he drive?"

"A black sports car."

Great. But then she wondered why she hadn't seen the car park somewhere behind them, or even pass them by. She'd looked because she'd hoped they could flag down someone to help them when Emma ran into Ruric.

"Clarissa's going to attend the rest of the school year with you. She has decided she would rather do that than homeschool now."

"Oh?" Instantly, Fiona became suspicious.

"Yeah," Clarissa said, her cheerful expression back in place. "We can do homework and have lunches together. It'll be great fun."

Fiona felt Clarissa was being assigned as an informer. Watch everything she does and report back to the head honcho. But Fiona wasn't sure if that was her great aunt now or Tobias.

"What do your parents think of you going to public high school?" Fiona asked, and finished the last bite of her spicy spaghetti. She had to admit, despite her great aunt's other shortcomings, she was a great cook.

"Tobias suggested it, really."

"He's your dad?" Fiona couldn't help the surprise in her voice.

Clarissa giggled. "No, he's my...uncle."

Right. Just like he was Fiona's. Just too eerie.

"Do you know anything about factorials, greatest common factors, or least common denominators? I've got some algebra homework to do."

"Sorry, I don't have a head for math. I have to run. See you both later."

Clarissa fairly skipped out of the room, then Fiona faced Regina. She was chewing the inside of her cheek like she did when she was contemplating something.

"What did you hear last night?" her great aunt asked.

Back to that. "Some guy wanted some girl. The girl needed to reject him. If she didn't, she needed to be killed."

For a second, her great aunt sat in morbid silence, then she laughed out loud. "Your mother always said you had a vivid imagination."

Her mother had never talked to Fiona or Justin, for that matter, about a Great Aunt Regina. Why wouldn't she have?

"Which teacher called you?" Fiona took her dish into the kitchen. She had to know which teacher was keeping an eye on her at school, just in case some nice guy got interested in Fiona, and she ratted on her to her great aunt about that too. Fiona felt as though she was living in some gigantic fishbowl and everyone was keeping an eye on her.

"Mrs. Emerson."

Fiona sighed deeply. She didn't know any Mrs. Emerson. "What subject does she teach?"

"Not sure, dear. Here, let me clean the dish. You never do this right."

Fiona did just fine cleaning dishes at home. Not with Regina. Everything had to be done just so. Fine with Fiona. It got her out of doing the dishes.

"I'll just go and do my homework. Oh, and I would really like to have a blue comforter in my room."

"Why?"

"Uhm, because it's my favorite color? Besides green. But for my room I would love blue. I'm not that fond of black."

"Maybe later, dear."

That meant no. But Fiona wasn't giving up.

"Oh, and, Great Aunt Regina—"

"Regina, dear," her great aunt said, her words biting.

Between clenched teeth, Fiona said, "Okay, Regina. The guy I was supposed to avoid, what was his name?"

Her great aunt stared at her as if she'd been hit with the strangest question.

"I didn't ask his name when he danced with me, and he didn't offer it," Fiona clarified, feeling like an idiot for not insisting he give her his name. From the sounds of it, she now had the reason why he had asked her to dance. He was bad news.

Regina nodded. "Arman Powe. Let me know if you see him again."

It had been Arman! Had he been fixated on her since that

day when she'd spilled her soda on him? But followed her all the way here? Two years later?

"Sure." But Fiona figured that was going to be Clarissa's job.

"And, Fiona." Regina said it as a way to get her attention.

"Yes?" Fiona paused at the kitchen entrance.

"My nephew, who was supposed to be your father, wasn't."

7

Pacing across the living room of the house they had rented, Arman was still furious with Ruric for jumping in front of Fiona's car and getting hit. Usually when he got mad at one of his friends, he would easily get over it. But he couldn't help feeling a grudge toward Ruric. What if Fiona had fallen for Ruric instead? Arman was supposed to be taking care of her, not Ruric. "Why did you pull what you did with Fiona?"

"I was trying to help you."

"I don't need your help. Here you had the opportunity to grab her then and you didn't." Arman glowered at Levka. "Or *you* could have." Arman sat down to have breakfast, Caitlin and Jasmine making ham and cheese omelets for them. Though the Scottish estate had a human chef, sometimes Arman and his friends swapped off on who made what meals for the day while the chef could go into town and buy supplies. And when they were on their own like this, they took turns.

Levka said, "Fiona can't be *forced* to do anything. If we had tried to get her to go into the house against her will, she could have screamed bloody murder and what a scene that would have made."

Arman had to admit Levka was right, though he wouldn't admit it out loud. He glanced at Caitlin. "You look a little pale today."

"Yeah, I'm having a cocktail with my breakfast."

Arman nodded. That was the trouble with having a more newly turned vampire in their little group.

"What are your plans for today?" Levka asked Arman.

"I'm going to the high school as a new student," Arman said.

"Me too," Stasio said.

"Though going to school doesn't appeal to me in the least, if Stasio is in, I'm in. Besides, a woman might be able to talk to Fiona when you guys could be seen as more of a threat," Jasmine said.

"Like I said, I'm joining you also," Caitlin said. "It would be great if we could become Fiona's new best girlfriends."

Levka swore. "I'm supposed to be Ruric's older brother. I can't go to school."

"We'll protect Caitlin," Ruric said.

"Absolutely. All of us were watching her back during the overthrow of the old Scottish League," Jasmine said. "Besides, I'm a vampire assassin. I can help. With Caitlin's special skills, she can too."

Arman knew Levka wasn't happy about the turn of events at all. He didn't blame him, but Levka had decided to be the big brother for this mission and Ruric had already explained that to Fiona and her friend so there was no changing their minds unless—

Levka snapped his fingers. "I'm just one of you. I'll change their memories of that moment when Ruric said I was his older brother."

"You can do that with Fiona's girlfriend because she's human, but Fiona is a hunter," Arman reminded him. "So you won't be able to change her mind."

"I'm going. I'll come up with something else then. Ruric, get us enrolled in school," Levka said.

Not in a million years did Arman think he and his friends would be going to a high school as students.

Ruric was on his computer, clacking away at the keyboard. "Okay, what assignments does everyone want to take?"

"What classes is Fiona in?" Arman asked.

"You can't be in all her classes," Jasmine warned. "We should split them up so some of us are in each of her classes."

Ruric smiled. "I'm on it."

"You're not related to my nephew, Avery Wilder, you know," Regina said again to Fiona, as if the words hadn't sunk in, which they hadn't.

Fiona's legs felt like they'd turned to boneless chicken, and she leaned against the doorjamb into the kitchen. Could her great aunt be losing it? Sure, she had the new face and not a bad body for being an older person, but there was nothing to turn back the aging brain.

"Yep. My nephew was the town drunk. The only good thing he ever did was got plenty of life insurance to take care of you and your brother. But he wasn't your father."

Fiona barely made it to the kitchen chair and slumped on the black velvet seat.

"Your mother, well, how can I put this delicately?"

Fiona's heart thundered. Her mother couldn't have had an affair with another man.

"I don't blame her at all. Avery was a difficult person to live with whether he was drinking or not. And Tobias, well, you've got to admit he's a charmer."

A charmer. Fiona's stomach churned with nausea. "You're not saying—"

"He's not your uncle. He's your father. We just didn't know how to break the news to you."

Fiona really didn't believe this. "And Justin's father?"

"No. Justin really is Avery's son. You're Justin's half-sister. Which means you and I are still related, if you have the notion we're not."

"Not by blood."

Regina cast her a hint of a smile.

Then Fiona's heart sank. "Tobias doesn't want me to live with him, does he?"

"I'm not getting any younger and he wants to get to know you better now that your parents are no longer here."

Fiona did *not* want to hear this. "Why didn't anyone tell me this before?"

"Your mother didn't want to tell you or my nephew the truth. I'm sure you can understand why. And my nephew never knew the truth. Neither did your brother."

"So how did *you* know?" Fiona couldn't believe her mother would tell Regina any of this. What if Regina had told her nephew and he had blown up at Fiona's mother?

"Timing. Avery was gone for two months to a rehab center, though it hadn't done any good, and Tobias moved in."

"I don't remember him."

Regina smiled. "You were being conceived. Your mother kept Tobias informed of what was going on with you over the years."

"Where does Tobias live?" Fiona still couldn't believe it.

"For now, you'll remain here with me. But your father wants you to have more restrictions."

"More?" Fiona couldn't help how shrill her voice had become. The Halloween party was the first time she'd been out since she'd moved here! More restrictions?

She wanted to scream.

"For one thing, he doesn't want you going out with Arman."

"Arman? I've never been out with anyone since I moved here. You know that."

"The guy you danced with at the party last night?"

"Oh."

"Your father doesn't like him or his family. Arman's attempting to see you to stir up trouble. Like I said, he has issues with stalking a girl if he gets obsessed with her."

Fiona knew it. There wasn't any other reason for him to be interested in her. Now she wondered if he'd actually tracked her down here, but it had taken all this time to do it. "You don't have to worry about it. He didn't bother to tell me his name even. Now that I know he's bad news, I won't have anything to do with him."

"He'll come back for you. It's a long-standing feud. Without fail, he'll return."

Fiona frowned. So she wasn't truly some random girl he was interested in? Figured. "What's the feud about? And what's Clarissa's relationship with...with..." Fiona couldn't call him her father. "Tobias."

"He's her...guardian."

Fiona didn't believe it for a minute. "Where are her parents? Does she have any other family?"

"All dead." Regina smiled one of her pasted-on smiles. "Tobias is all she has. As for the feud, it goes back centuries."

"Centuries?"

"Figure of speech, dear. Why don't you run along and do your homework?"

All Fiona could think about was Arman, the stalker, and Ruric, the guy they'd run over with Emma's car, who she thought was a friend of Arman's. Had all that been staged?

Though, Ruric truly had been...well, nearly dead, and she didn't think that could have been part of the plan to see her.

THE NEXT DAY AT SCHOOL, Fiona had wanted to see Ruric and hoped he was still alright after they ran into him with the car and learn what was going on with him and Arman being here, if Ruric actually managed to change schools. Clarissa, however, accompanied her, and that really bothered her. It wouldn't have if she hadn't felt that the girl was going to report back to Tobias and Regina about all that went on with Fiona at school.

Luckily, Clarissa wasn't in Fiona's first class. Fiona walked into history class, not thinking of anything really, except she had a test next week. That's when she saw Tux—Arman—and nearly had a heart attack. He was sitting right next to her desk, as if he knew that was her assigned seat.

"Everyone take a seat," Mrs. Johnson said to Fiona, since she was the only student in class who was standing there, her mouth agape. She snapped it shut, felt chills creeping up her spine, and took her seat.

"I'm Arman," he whispered to her.

She ignored him and tried to listen to what the teacher had to say, but she was having an awful time of it. What happened next surprised her even more. Ruric entered the class and raised his brows at Arman. He *did* know him! Just like she had suspected. Arman just shook his head at Ruric.

Then Ruric looked at the teacher, who opened her mouth to speak. She paused, and then she said, "Ramon, please move to the seat in the back of the class. Thank you. Ruric, you can take Ramon's seat."

A shuffling of seats ensued, and then Fiona was sitting between the two guys who'd been wearing tuxes last night—the one who Emma had run over with her mother's car, and the other who had tried to steal Fiona away from the dance. She didn't hear a thing the teacher said after that, knowing these guys meant real trouble for her.

Ruric passed a note to her.

She opened it up. *What is your birth date?* She glanced at him. He smiled.

She wrote on the note: *How do you know Arman?*

As soon as she passed the note to him, the teacher caught the action. Certain she would get chewed out, her cheeks warmed. Instead, the teacher gazed at Ruric, nodded, and continued with her lesson.

Arman is like a brother to me, Ruric wrote back.

She stared at the teacher, not believing she would ignore Ruric. *Arman is a brother like Levka is to you?* she wrote back, frowning.

He handed the note back to her. *You're in danger.*

She eyed him, not believing her great aunt would say the same thing to her about Arman. Now Ruric, who was like a brother to him, gave her the very same warning?

Because of Arman? she asked, hoping Arman didn't catch sight of the note.

Because of Tobias.

Her heart skipped a beat. She didn't trust Tobias one bit, but now she didn't know what to think. Had Ruric risked his life by stepping out in front of the car to speak with her and befriend her, because he was worried about her? Or was he in league with Arman? The stalker? And possible ex-girlfriend murderer?

We don't know what Regina has told you, but we need to talk to you. We saw Clarissa here. She's bad news. She doesn't know we're here yet, but if she learns we are, she'll report back to Tobias at once, Ruric wrote.

Fiona did what she never did when she was in class—she got

up and walked out of the classroom. Her heart was beating way too fast, and she didn't trust these guys any more than she trusted her great aunt, Clarissa, or the man who said he was her father. She really didn't believe any of it. She *wasn't* surprised when both Ruric and Arman headed out of the class after her.

"Okay, listen," Arman said, "you're in grave danger."

And it wasn't even Halloween any longer!

∽

REGINA AND TOBIAS were cunning vampires, and they might have persuaded Fiona that Arman was bad news.

He understood Fiona's disbelief. She felt she had no one to turn to, no one to trust. Even though Arman and his friends saw themselves as vampires who did good, the League of Vampires in some locations thought otherwise.

"Listen," Arman said, "I came to protect you from them."

"You staged the accident, so it looked like we'd killed you?" she asked Ruric, ignoring Arman's comment and sounding outraged.

"No. I was trying to get your friend's attention. She hit me before she saw me and before I could get out of the way," Ruric said.

"Regina said you were stalking a girl and then she ended up mysteriously dead," Fiona said to Arman.

"She lies. I don't have any girlfriends, nor have I tried to make any. I don't even attend high school," Arman said, defending himself.

"Then why are you here? Ohmigod, what is going on?" Fiona wanted to call the police, but she knew they wouldn't believe her about any of this. And if Arman hadn't killed any girl, there would be no record of it either.

"To protect you. There are more of us. Jasmine, Caitlin,

Levka, and Stasio. We're all here trying to make sure they don't harm you," Arman said.

"Arman came swooping in to save you, without wanting our help. We came with him to make sure Tobias, or the others, didn't kill him," Ruric said. "They mean to steal your power before the blood moon and your eighteenth birthday."

"I shouldn't be missing class," Fiona finally said, trying to rationalize that these two guys were crazy, and she should be in class where she could be safer. "Wait, what do you mean I have powers?"

"You're supposed to be a hunter, but you can telepathically communicate with me." They needed to get her out of there now, but Arman knew if they tried, she would believe she was being kidnapped by a couple of really weird dudes.

"What?" she asked.

"When you were in your bedroom last night. I was trying to get you to let me in," Arman said. "We were talking...*like this.*" He realized she would think he had just spoken to her out loud. So he tried again. *"My lips aren't moving. I'm talking to you telepathically now."*

Fiona laughed. "Oh, you're a ventriloquist."

"Look at me," Ruric said. *"We are talking to you telepathically."*

"We're coming," Jasmine said. *"I just got a bathroom break. The same with Caitlin. Where are you guys? In Fiona's classroom or outside of it?"*

"By the bathrooms near her classroom," Arman said.

Fiona was staring at him. Yep, Jasmine's talking inside of Fiona's head got her attention.

Then Jasmine and Caitlin were hurrying down the hallway to meet up with them. "I'm Jasmine," she said, offering her hand.

Fiona didn't shake it.

"Caitlin," Caitlin said. "We really need to get out of here before Clarissa learns what we're up to."

"What are you up to?" Fiona asked.

Stasio and Levka soon joined them. Levka said, "Saving you from vampires who want you either to join them or they intend to kill you. You're cursed and we need to learn how to break it before they can use it for their own good."

8

"I don't know you, *any* of you," Fiona said, her heart racing. This was all just a new nightmare to her.

"Once they learn we're here to protect you," Stasio said, "Regina and Tobias will make sure you never return to school. They'll keep you locked up and guarded at all times."

Arman swept Fiona up in his arms and vanished.

Fiona didn't know what had just happened. One minute she was standing in the hallway of her school, talking to a bunch of teens she didn't know who said they were intent on saving her, and then she was in a black void and now lying on a couch in a house she didn't recognize.

Appearing genuinely worried about her, Arman frowned as he stood next to the couch, looking down at her. "I'm sorry. I had to do that so that we could talk privately and before Clarissa learned we were there. I didn't kill some girl at a high school. And I've never been a stalker. They made it all up, afraid I would show up to try and protect you."

Then the others arrived, and she just stared at them. They weren't there, then they were, like a transporter beam had transported them there without the spaceship, weird transporter sounds, or bright, glittery lights.

"Regina, Tobias, and Clarissa are vampires. Ruthless kinds," Arman said. "They believe you have an ability they can exploit."

"Vampires? You can't be serious. And for your information, I don't have any powers." Fiona rubbed her forehead. "What are you then? You just appeared before me like magic."

"We're vampires also," Arman said. "But we're the good guys. We help humans or hunters or vampires in need. Tobias only wants power. We came here, well, I came here to help you because I've been having visions and dreams of you and you're in the worst kind of danger. In the visions, I'm there, saving you. But then a blond-haired man had also come to me and warned me that I had to protect you before the blood moon. My friends came also to assist me and you. I know it's a lot to take in all at once, but it's the truth."

Fiona folded her arms. "I won't believe any of this unless you prove it to me."

Arman exposed his long, sharp canines. Fiona gaped at the sight of them, then she closed her mouth. They had to be fake. Though he hadn't talked as though he had some kind of pretend extended fangs that might affect his speech. Of course, some went as far as to actually have vampire fang implants that were permanent. She glanced at the others. "Well?"

Levka gave her a smile, showing his off. Perfectly wicked looking. But she didn't accept that any of this was real. Were they members of some cult who had dental work to make them appear to have vampire fangs to live the life as "vampires?" Not real ones, of course.

Ruric and Stasio showed off theirs. And then Jasmine went next. But Caitlin wasn't showing hers off.

"I saved Caitlin's life," Levka explained. "She's more newly turned so showing off her fangs isn't something she has had a lot of control over."

"But I'm a witch also, and that makes up for what I lack in the vampire department," Caitlin said, turning herself invisible and then visible again.

If Fiona had had something to drink or eat here, she might have thought she was hallucinating. "Open your mouths."

Everyone did, but the fangs were gone. She blinked—twice.

"We conceal them. We normally only show them off when we're angry or in a fight," Arman said. "There's no need to otherwise. Except for show and tell."

"Or to drink someone's blood," she said.

"We have our own vampire blood banks," Ruric explained. "Humans donate their blood, we pay them for it, but no one even knows that vampires are using it. Everyone's happy."

"You're not going to drink my blood?" Fiona asked, thinking back to the curse. They might get sick or something if they drank her blood, if any of this was true.

"No. We're here to save you, but I think we ought to be leaving," Arman said.

The others all looked at him and she swore something was being communicated between them, but she wasn't getting the message. "I'm still in the room."

"Will you go with us? The blood moon is nearly here, just a few days away. That's when they will convince you to be one of them, or they'll eliminate you," Arman said.

That made her think back to what Tobias and Regina had been talking about earlier.

Stasio disappeared and reappeared with a book.

"We normally don't do that," Ruric said, motioning to Stasio. "We just walk into the next room and bring the book back here."

"Time is of the essence," Stasio said. "That girl who was supposed to be watching out for you will soon learn you're not at school and report back to Tobias and Regina. They will call up their people to locate you."

"People. The others at the Halloween party who disappeared so strangely," Fiona said. None of it still made any sense, but maybe that's why Regina and the others seemed so...strange. "What about my brother, Justin?"

"He's dead. They killed him and your parents," Arman said.

Tears filled Fiona's eyes. "No."

"Yes," Levka said. "Arman is telling you the truth. They had to get you away from your family."

"Regina lied about all of it, the car accident, leaving out the part that your brother isn't alive either," Arman said.

Fiona quickly wiped away tears.

Then everyone looked at Levka and she swore they were talking to each other in secret again.

Fiona let out her breath in a huff. "I'm *still* in the room."

"We're going to take you somewhere safe until we can leave for a place even farther away. Once the blood moon has passed, you'll be safe," Levka said.

"You're planning to take me where?" Fiona asked.

"Dallas," Arman said.

"Don't tell me, we have to leave our luggage behind," Jasmine said, sounding exasperated.

"We each have backpacks. Hurry and pack what you can in those and we'll leave," Levka said.

"What if I don't want to go with you?" Not that Fiona wanted to stay with Regina and Tobias, especially after hearing what these...vampires had to say about them, if it was all true—but what if it wasn't?

"You don't have to go with us," Jasmine said. "They saved my life too. I didn't have to go with them, but it was either that and help watch their backs as they watched mine or fend for myself on my own. I'm known as a vampire assassin, so I can usually take care of myself. I eliminate rogue vampires. But I wouldn't have made it on my own that time. They didn't take me with them because they had to. They did it because they wanted to keep me safe."

"Dallas is where—" Fiona hesitated to finish her words. She thought her brother was at the college there. "Are you sure my brother is dead?"

Stasio disappeared and reappeared, handing her a newspaper. "I'm the historian of the bunch, but I also researched all about you when Arman said he was having visions of you."

She glanced again at Arman. She remembered vague visions, surreal, oddball dreams, nightmares too, and Arman looked like the man of those dreams. And she remembered more—kissing him and feeling safe in his arms. "Alright, but when we get to Dallas, I want to speak to the police about my brother."

"We can certainly make arrangements for that," Levka said.

"What about *my* clothes?" Fiona asked, as the others packed their backpacks.

"You can use our money to buy whatever you need when we reach our destination," Levka said.

Then, before she was ready to move again, Arman wrapped his arms around her. "We'll be stopping a few times because it's too far to travel in a day for us."

"Next stop, Nevada," Levka said, and then they all vanished.

They were flying, Fiona realized, but she couldn't see anyone or herself even. They were just soaring above the world, the wind in their faces, clouds cloaking them, Arman's arms around her, keeping her safe.

"Caitlin made us invisible so that we can fly without anyone seeing us," Arman said. "Normally, we would only fly at night. Another thing we need to mention to you. Your family—mother, father, and brother—weren't blood relations."

"What?" The story kept changing. Okay, so Regina had told Fiona that her father hadn't been her father, and her brother was a half brother, but she'd said her mother was her mother. "Regina told me my father wasn't really my father, but my mother was really my mother."

"Regina lied."

Fiona didn't know what to believe anymore. "She said Tobias was my father."

"Another lie. Tobias isn't either," Arman said again. "And Regina isn't related to you at all."

"I didn't believe Tobias was. Regina? I'm glad she's not. But my mother and Justin?" This was just too unreal. Yet Fiona had often thought that she didn't look like anyone in the family, her mother, father, and brother having had dark hair and eyes while she had blond hair and green eyes.

"No. He wasn't any relation to you, and the woman who claimed she was your mother wasn't either," Arman said. "You were placed with the family for safekeeping."

"My father, or the man pretending to be my father, was a drunk. He beat my mother. How would my real parents have thought that was a safe place for me to grow up? Wait, so if my parents placed me with them, are they alive?" Fiona hoped that she still had a family.

"It's possible. We'll use every resource available to us to learn the truth," Arman said. "I don't know why they would have picked that particular family to be your foster parents. They probably didn't know about your foster father's alcohol problem and other abuses."

Fiona didn't entirely trust these people.

Then Arman started explaining how he and the other guys with him had been turned into vampires by the Black Death, but that some had survived as humans, and others were hunters of rogue vampires.

"But Jasmine is a vampire, and she hunts vampires," Fiona said, at least so they said.

"Right." Arman explained about the League of Vampires in various places in the States and also around the world.

When they finally arrived in Nevada, they stayed at a five-star hotel in Las Vegas, and this was where it got kind of dicey. Arman wanted to stay with Fiona. She wasn't staying with anyone but a female. Caitlin was obviously with Levka who had mentioned saving her life, and Fiona could see that Stasio was with Jasmine. But both ladies said they would stay with her and keep her safe.

Fiona was glad for it. She hadn't ever had a decent relationship with a guy before and she wasn't going to jump into one like this when she still wasn't sure about these people. They were vampires! What if Arman wanted to feed off her in the middle of the night? At least she thought she would feel safer with Caitlin and Jasmine.

Fiona suddenly remembered that she had left Emma behind without a word that she was going to disappear. "What about my friend?" She felt terrible that she'd forgotten all about Emma.

"We were in her class," Jasmine said, "and we convinced her that you didn't exist."

"What?"

"You can't go back there. It's too dangerous for you." Jasmine abruptly changed the topic. "Let's go. We need to shop and pick up what you need in the line of clothes and personal items."

"They had to do the same thing with my foster parents and foster sister," Caitlin told Fiona, sounding sympathetic. "That way no one's looking for us, thinking we were kidnapped, or were just runaways."

"What about school?" All this was just sinking in for Fiona.

"I am taking advanced college-level witch's training," Caitlin said. "All online. We can find an online curriculum for you too. Regular education, of course. Not witch's training."

"The Black Death was a long time ago. How long have you been with them?" Fiona asked them as they found a shop to go into that had extravagantly-priced jeans and jackets—really high dollar items. She was going to leave, but Jasmine stopped her.

"We're independently wealthy. Pick out whatever you want. I was born a vampire. I wasn't turned. I'm not as old as the guys." Jasmine eyed a leather jacket.

"Wait, if you were born a vampire, how come you aged? Wouldn't you have been a newborn always?" Fiona asked, so perplexed about all of this.

"We age normally like humans until we're between eighteen and twenty-one and then our aging process slows way down," Jasmine said.

"What...what if a hunter and vampire have a baby? Or is that even possible?" Fiona asked.

"I've heard they're daylight vampires, unaffected by the sun, except like a human who could be burned, don't need blood, have all the powers of a hunter and vampire combined," Jasmine said.

"Oh, I never even thought of that. I was turned last year, so I'm new at all this still," Caitlin said. "Be sure to pack up a bathing suit or two. They have a beautiful indoor pool that you can enjoy. Can you swim?"

"Oh, yes. That would be great."

After Fiona picked out a few pairs of jeans, a couple of jackets, panties, bras, socks, five shirts, a sweater, a couple of skirts, a dress, two bathing suits, flip flops, a robe, pajamas, and another pair of boots, Jasmine paid for them. Fiona didn't *even* want to see how much all that cost her.

Then they returned to the hotel room, and everyone met up at Fiona's room to have pizzas delivered.

Fiona had never paid that much for clothes ever. She was kind of liking her new group of friends. Even the spacious suite they had was gorgeous, all light and airy, not dark and depressing like her—well, Regina's home. Since Regina wasn't really any relation to Fiona, in reality, the woman had stolen her and taken her to Oregon under false pretenses.

"You were going to show me a book," Fiona said as their meals were delivered.

"Yeah." Stasio handed it to her. "You won't be able to read the language. It's ancient Welsh, but this tells all about the earlier family lines. Ruric, Levka, Arman, and I are all Welsh princes. We're listed here. All the families have their own books, but some have been uploaded online in this new electronic age."

"That's where I come in," Ruric said. "When Arman said he was having the visions of you, we researched who the vampires were who had taken you from your foster family. We're still trying to learn who your real parents are."

"What about the...curse?" If Fiona was to believe any of this.

"You come into an ability that has to do with dreams when the blood moon is full and you reach your eighteenth birthday," Stasio said. "Both are a few days away. I mean, some say it's a curse because there will be rogue vampires who will be after you for your power, but it might be something that really benefits you if you can learn how to harness it."

"When we get to Dallas, I want to see the police," Fiona reiterated, not buying this curse business. She thought that the vampires truly believed in it, but she couldn't see that having dreams made her powerful. If she didn't have any control over her life right now, at least she had to know what had happened to her foster brother. She still cared for him and didn't want to give up hope that he was alive.

"Yes. We'll give you the time to check on your brother. But we can't take too long," Arman warned. "They'll be looking for you and they might believe you would try to go there, if they suspect you want to be with your brother."

Which was just what Fiona had told Regina. That wasn't good. "I can't believe Justin wasn't my real brother. How can we learn more about my family?"

"I'll be searching all the archives I can find to try and locate them. In the meantime, you have to stay with us, and we'll protect you," Stasio said.

"What if *you* want whatever 'powers' I might have just like Tobias and Regina?" Fiona wasn't dumb. If one group of vampires wanted them, then another could want them also.

"We help others in need. We've gotten in trouble for it also," Levka said. "If we just didn't stick our noses into other people's business, we wouldn't have any concerns."

"Why would you be in trouble for doing something good for people?" Fiona didn't think it made any sense.

"Vampire League rules. No helping humans or hunters even when they're innocent of any wrongdoing and need our help," Levka said.

"That's awful." Fiona couldn't believe it. "So you're telling me you're good Samaritan vampires then."

"Yeah, we are," Arman said. "Though you should know that I tend to remind everyone of the rules so they don't get into as much of a hassle."

"Does that mean with regard to coming to rescue me also?" Fiona asked.

"Are you kidding? He was going to help you whether any of us wanted to come or not," Levka said.

Fiona smiled at him. "Thanks." Then she lost the smile. "I think." Though a part of her was relieved that she wouldn't have to return to Regina's house and see Tobias or Clarissa either, she still wasn't certain going with these people was a step in the right direction.

"We need to get some sleep. We leave in four hours." Levka took Caitlin's hand, and they left the room.

"We'll be in the room next door." Arman pointed to the adjoining door. "Just call on us if you need any help."

"We will." Jasmine kissed Stasio and he kissed her back.

Fiona was thinking about how they should really be together, but she guessed she'd really messed that up for them. Maybe at the next place they stayed, they could get an extra room and they could be together. She also noticed that Levka had spirited Caitlin away even though she'd said she would stay with Fiona and Jasmine.

Fiona got a call and when she looked at the caller ID, she realized it was Regina and her heart began beating like crazy.

Everyone still in the room was watching her.

"Regina," Fiona whispered, as if she could hear her through the phone when she hadn't even answered the call. "What if she can track me through my phone?"

"This is not good," Arman said. *"Levka, none of us thought about Fiona's cell phone. Regina just called her."*

"Aww, hell—" Levka said then, *"Let's go. We'll drop the phone in someone's vehicle on the way out."*

Then Arman said, "We've got to pack right now and move."

"I'm sorry. I never thought I would be on the run from vampire rogues." Fiona shook her head. "I heard...heard Levka talking."

"Yes. You heard his telepathic communication," Arman said.

Okay, so Fiona guessed she really could hear their communication that way.

It didn't take long for everyone to pack, and no one argued about it either. Fiona was surprised how well the group worked together.

Then they headed outside into the dark and Levka found an

unlocked car door. He slipped the phone inside and locked the door and shut it. "Let's go."

The next thing she knew, they were flying again, invisible, and she didn't think she would ever get used to this. *"Where are we going now?"* She thought of each of the vampires and hoped they would all hear her.

"Sedona, Arizona," Levka said. *"We'll stop there for four hours. After that, we're on the move again."*

"Okay, I can't make reservations while we're flying," Ruric said. *"When we land, I'll do it."*

"When you do, make reservations for Las Cruces, New Mexico after that," Levka said.

"Gotcha," Ruric said.

"When I talk to you, are you all hearing me?" Fiona asked.

"Yeah," Ruric said, everyone else agreeing.

"But we need to know if you can talk to only one person or several in the group," Arman said. *"When Caitlin telepathically speaks, she can't target individuals."*

"Alright, I'm speaking only to you, Arman. Thanks for saving me from Regina and the others."

"You're welcome," he said.

"Did anyone else hear what I said to Arman?" Fiona asked.

"Not me," Jasmine said, everyone echoing her response.

Then Fiona tried to speak only to Jasmine and Caitlin. *"Thank you, Jasmine and Caitlin, for saying you would share a room with me."* Though Levka seemed to have the final say in that. *"If... if we can't get more rooms this time at the next stop, why don't the two of you stay with your boyfriends?"*

"Someone has to stay with you," Jasmine said.

"Jasmine's right. You can't be alone in case Regina, or her cohorts, catch up to us," Caitlin said.

"We only heard Caitlin's response, no one else's conversations,"

Levka said. *"It appears you can direct your telepathic conversation to only those you wish to speak to."* He sounded relieved.

"Great," Fiona said. At least one good thing was going for her, besides being rescued from Tobias and Regina. She just hoped Arman and his friends truly were decent vampires and not conning her like Regina had done.

9

When they reached their next destination, Ruric managed to get them enough rooms and a honeymoon suite so that Arman and Fiona had a living room and a bedroom with two queen size beds. That meant Ruric had a room of his own, but they couldn't risk Fiona staying alone in a room.

"I'll sleep on the sofa," Arman offered, being the gallant prince that he was.

"Okay, thanks," Fiona said.

Arman had hoped she would be fine with him staying in the other bed in the same room, but that was the difference between Stasio and Jasmine. Both of them were vampires. Fiona was probably still afraid any one of them would want to suck her blood while she was sleeping.

Humans could be compelled to do things, but as a hunter, she couldn't be. He smiled at her, willing her to invite him into the bedroom to take the other bed while she slept in the one by the window. He reassured her she would have the most wonderful sleep, just in case they were wrong about her being a huntress.

She smiled at him, like she thought he had something else in mind. A kiss? He could just see going in for a kiss goodnight and getting attacked by a black belt in some form of martial arts.

He was the one known for not taking big risks in their little group. But then he decided to throw caution to the wind and drew close. She was looking wary, but tired too. Then he pulled her gently in for a kiss, hoping she didn't knee him where it counted.

To his surprise, relief, and delight, she kissed him before he even had a chance to kiss her. He had a lot of experience and he suspected she didn't have, but when she kissed him, he felt a strange kind of connection, like they belonged together and the visions he'd had of her had prepared him for this moment.

He was really getting into the kiss when she pulled away, her face flushed, her breathing hard, her heart beating rapidly.

"Why...why does it feel like I've known you forever?" she asked.

"I don't know. I felt the same kind of emotional and physical attraction to you." And he couldn't believe it.

Levka said to both Arman and Fiona, *"Go to sleep before we have to leave again. Talk to each other tomorrow."*

Fiona's eyes widened.

Arman said, "He's only guessing we're talking or something. He can't read our minds. Night, Fiona. We'll talk later." Then he gave her a warm hug, kissed her briefly, and left her alone in the bedroom.

"Wait," she said. "You can use the other bed. Otherwise, you'll have to waste time making up a bed on the couch."

"Okay, thanks." He was going to ask her if she was sure, but he didn't want to sabotage the offer.

Then they all settled down before they had to leave again. Arman was hoping that the phone they had left in a vehicle was headed in an altogether different direction from where they were headed.

"It won't be safe going to Dallas to check on what happened to my brother, will it?" Fiona asked Arman after she slipped under her covers.

"Probably not. But if you have to do it, we'll understand." Arman rested his head on his pillow.

"Regina will call on reinforcements and you'll be outnumbered. We can't risk that. I can check newspaper reports later, right?" she asked.

Relieved, he said, "Sure."

"If they were able to track the phone to our last location, I'm worried they'll think we're going this way."

"Right. We can talk to the others when we get ready to leave," Arman said.

"Or now, so everyone can make other plans. I'll do it," Fiona said. "It's my decision to take a different route."

"It's a good decision." Arman was glad she wasn't feeling shy about bothering Levka, though he was a bit amused. *He didn't like bothering Levka when he retired to bed with Caitlin unless it was a dire emergency. Well, even before Caitlin was with him.*

Then Fiona said to everyone, *"Hey, if it works for you, let's go to somewhere other than Dallas. Regina might figure that's where I would want to go."*

"How about Houston?" Levka asked.

"That works for me," Fiona said.

Everyone chimed in that that was a good plan. *"I'll make the reservations for the hotel,"* Ruric said.

Then they went to sleep, but only for a short while. Not long after that, Levka was waking them for lunch and then another flight.

"I just thought about another thing. Regina knew your name, Arman. How did she know you would come after me?"

Fiona asked, while they had lunch in the suite—Chinese food this time.

"We know about her, but I don't know how she would know about me, unless she has had visions of your white knight coming to save you," Arman said.

Fiona laughed.

He liked her laughter. He liked dancing with her too. And she was really pretty. He liked blondes and her enchanting green eyes always captured him and drew him in—now, when he finally got to see her in person again, and in the visions and dreams he'd had of her.

He was glad she had changed the plan so that they now avoided Dallas because he knew everyone had been worried about going there in case Regina figured they were heading to that location.

"Where are we going after this?" Fiona asked.

"We're flying to another country."

Fiona frowned. "I don't have a passport. Which country?"

"Scotland. We can take care of the passport issue," Levka said. "Our vampiric persuasion is very...persuasive."

"That comes in handy then."

"It does," Caitlin said. "Before I met these guys, I couldn't have done half of all the things we've done—the hotel reservations, flight reservations, even purchasing the meals, and clothes. So they can make sure that you bypass the passport issue. We often get first class seats on the planes too. But it means that we bump people out of their seats sometimes. I... well, I didn't think I would like being like that, but you know those people always have the wealth, first class everything. So it doesn't hurt for them to live like the common man every once in a while."

Fiona smiled. "Yeah, I know what you mean. I have another idea. It might be kind of absurd, but can we go to Moody

Gardens on Galveston Island? I've always wanted to go but my parents wouldn't take us, and my brother never wanted to go. No way would Regina or the others suspect I would drop by there. Nor that if Arman 'stole' me, that he would take me there."

"Moody Gardens it is," Levka said.

Arman said, "If they access the worldwide registry of important vampires, then they would know I'm from Wales. But we're not going there. They would have to dig a lot further to learn where we might be living now. That should take time and we have a lot of friends there who will back us up." He sighed. "As to Moody Gardens, unless you mentioned to Regina or the others that you always wanted to go to that location, she might make a trip there or send people you don't know there. Otherwise, it should be safe."

"No, I mentioned I wanted to go to Dallas to the university to join my brother. I don't know if he would have been okay with it, but that was what I had planned to do. I guess all of that's out now."

"Online courses," Caitlin said, smiling. "You can do the whole thing that way. Well, depending on what you want to study."

"I don't know yet. I'm sure whatever I would have planned will have to be changed considering the circumstances." Fiona hated uncertainty and this was more than she thought she would ever have to deal with. Having some control over her life was important, so being able to go to Moody Gardens gave her a tiny sense of having some say in her life. She didn't want to think about the blood moon, or her birthday, or about any powers she might end up having. She didn't really believe she could have any, truthfully.

She still didn't know if she could trust these vampires. She'd just met them and they'd taken her away from, well, people she thought she knew. She might think they were lying about her relationship with Regina and Tobias, but Fiona didn't believe Regina or Tobias had been telling her the truth either.

Maybe she was being silly about going to Moody Gardens, but everyone seemed to think the idea was perfectly fine, so she was glad for that.

"Okay, are we ready to go?" Levka asked. "We'll stay in Houston, and then travel to Galveston from there. It's only an hour away."

"Why not go straight to Galveston instead of stopping in Houston first?" Fiona hoped they didn't think she sounded like she was afraid they might change their minds and just get on a plane for Scotland in Houston.

"Sure," Levka said. "It's so close, that will work. Ruric?"

"On it," Ruric said.

When they arrived at the hotel on Galveston Island, they all went to their rooms—Caitlin staying with Fiona while they took turns showering, and then joined the rest of the gang to see Moody Gardens.

"So I was surprised you all eat food," Fiona finally mentioned.

"Yeah," Caitlin said. "So except for showing off fangs in anger, we look like any other human. Except, I'm also a witch."

"Also, there are hunters who were changed at the same time during the Black Death and their offspring. They don't have a craving for blood like we do. They're stronger like us, and it had been their goal to destroy vampires," Levka said. "Then things changed over the centuries and hunters began to realize not all vampires are bad. That some hunters are evil, killing machines. We try to police our own rogue vampires, though hunters are also hired to take care of the rogues."

"What about rogue hunters?" Fiona asked. "Who takes care of them?"

"The hunters," Ruric said. "The vampires have to report

them to a hunter council in the jurisdiction. Vampires aren't allowed to take down rogue hunters without being called rogues themselves."

"Wow, that doesn't sound fair," Fiona asked.

"No, it isn't," Arman said.

"Okay, so if hunters were also turned by the Black Death, did they live long lives also?" Fiona asked.

"Yeah, if they were turned by the plague. But their offspring didn't have that ability," Arman said.

"There's so much to remember. So what happens when I turn eighteen during the blood moon?" Fiona asked.

Stasio said, "Between my researching historical documents..."

"And my help with unraveling data online...," Ruric said.

"And me analyzing the dreams I've been having of you...," Arman said.

Levka cleared his throat. "We've learned you will have the ability to manipulate dreams—giving a targeted individual pleasant slumber, torment someone with nightmares, or even cause the person to sleepwalk and act out in some way."

"Like killing someone?"

Arman glanced at the others, and then back at Fiona. "Yeah. And Tobias and Regina and their clan want your ability to control others in their dream state."

"And you?"

Arman shook his head. "I only want what's best for you. If we can break the curse, then Tobias and Regina and their minions will no longer have any need to take you into the fold."

10

Fiona had finally found freedom from her crazy homelife and thought going to Moody Gardens would be fun before she left the States. But was she nuts to want to do this now? With Regina and Tobias probably trying to track them down?

Ruric was working his vampiric magic to pay for the expensive tickets, Arman was beside Fiona as they got their tickets, Levka and Caitlin were behind them, and Stasio and Jasmine beside them.

She wanted to ask Caitlin what powers a witch had but didn't want to sound too nosey. She figured she would learn about them soon enough. Then they headed into one of the glass pyramids featuring the rainforest. They saw beautiful orchids perched on trees and brilliantly colored macaws gathered together in pairs of blues, reds, and greens. Fish swam in the ponds and skates, similar to manta rays, glided across the water in the shadows. Alligators were in one area, fruit bats clung to manmade caves in another exhibit. Monkeys roamed free in the jungle of trees and vines. Other brightly colored tropical flowers that Fiona didn't know the name of filled pockets here and there.

Her next favorite thing was the butterfly exhibit and she reached into her pocket to grab her phone to take pictures of them, realizing at once she didn't have her phone. Arman, seeing her distress at being cut off from the world, pulled out his phone and handed it to her. "We'll get you one."

Tears filled her eyes. She didn't know why she'd suddenly become overcome with sadness. She was supposed to be enjoying herself for the moment, but it just hit her all at once. Here she was again, her whole world turned upside down from living with one dysfunctional foster family to another so to speak, and now? She was with a group of vampires who were probably just as dysfunctional, yet Arman's gesture to give her his phone, to show he was watching her, understanding how she felt, it just...well, it just had overwhelmed her all in that moment.

He reached over and pulled her into a hug then and she needed that. She'd needed it ever since she'd learned her parents, or foster parents, had died in the car crash. She'd needed to feel like she'd belonged somewhere with someone, not like how she'd lived with Regina for the last few months.

Then she realized another thing. She didn't have to go to school any longer! No more extra credit classes for social studies or attending dumb Halloween parties, no expectations of going to the prom when she probably wouldn't have been asked anyway. Though she wanted to graduate. But on her own terms. In her own way.

"Thank you," she belatedly said and took a picture of Arman, wondering if she could even take a picture of him.

He was smiling so brightly at her, she thought she'd made his day. Probably no one ever took his picture. She smiled back, the lighthearted feeling contagious. Then she began taking pictures of the butterflies, closeup, sitting on flowers, lingering on fruit. She made everyone go back through the rainforest so she could take pictures of the monkeys, macaws, and flowers and then they went to see the aquarium.

An octopus moved around coral, trying to hide from her. She knew the feeling, but she managed to capture a couple of good photos. An electric eel, a neon green, appeared just in time for a photo. Penguins were getting a meal of fish in the exhibit. Puffins were swimming in another area. Seals were likewise diving into the water in an exhibit. Walking through a glass tunnel surrounded by sharks and fish while divers were cleaning the glass was the coolest. Even seeing the different varieties of jellyfish was really fun. Or the sea stars and other sea life that she enjoyed capturing on the cell phone. Then she wondered what pictures Arman might have taken. She would check the first chance she got, when he wasn't aware of it, just in case he had taken some selfies with a cute girl.

She assumed everyone would have been annoyed with her for wanting to take so many pictures, but they had seemed glad to do whatever she wanted to do. Maybe because by doing so, she would agree to stay with them. Even though Jasmine said it was her choice, Fiona suspected that they wouldn't want to give her the freedom to decide to stay behind. Still, she appreciated that they were letting her do whatever she wanted to and seemed to be enjoying the time they spent with her. Unlike Regina who had never wanted to let her out of her sight except to go to school, normally. Until that Halloween high school party. Boy did Regina make a mistake then.

At the cafeteria, they all ordered pizzas and then sat down to eat them.

"I hope everyone is enjoying being here and it's not just me that is," Fiona said, thinking they were, but maybe they were just pretending.

"Oh, yeah, I've never been here either and I've had a ball. At least five morpho butterflies were traveling on the back of Levka's shirt. He really was attracting them. It was hilarious," Caitlin said.

Levka smiled at Caitlin.

Fiona knew then Caitlin was being honest with her and Levka seemed to enjoy anything that made Caitlin happy.

"I loved the monkeys too. And the macaws," Jasmine said. "With the kind of work I do, I never just take the time to sightsee, and I've never been to Texas before. So this was fun for me."

Jasmine sounded sincere also, and Fiona really liked both of them.

None of the guys said anything, so Fiona suspected they were worried about hanging around here for too long.

They had missed the ferry, which was probably just as well. Arman had told her they couldn't fly over big bodies of water, so if they'd had to leave in a hurry, they wouldn't have been able to.

Stasio handed Jasmine his phone and said, "I've been trying to learn anything I can about your foster brother, but I thought this was interesting. The news report should have mentioned he was survived by a sister, but there's no mention of you like you didn't even exist."

"Because...because like you wiped out Emma's memory of me, Regina made sure no one knew I had existed?" Fiona asked, astonished. Why worry about her ability to work some magic on people's dreams when they could wipe out people's memories all on their own?

"Right," Arman said, then took another bite of his pizza.

"But if I'm a hunter, then shouldn't they be afraid of me because I could eliminate them for being rogue vampires?" Fiona asked, trying to wrap her mind around this whole new world she'd found herself in.

"You haven't been raised as a hunter and trained as one, killing rogue vampires from an early age," Levka said.

"But I'm a black belt in several forms of martial arts, and I can wield a sword."

"Why?" Stasio asked. "How come you went into martial arts training?"

"My mother said I would love it. Ohmigod, because my real parents told her I should be trained in it? To eventually fight vampires? Rogue ones, I mean?" Fiona just couldn't come to grips with all this. She had done several sword demonstrations, but the idea of actually using one on someone to terminate him or her? She shuddered.

"Well, it's good to hear that you can wield a sword and you know martial arts. You'll be much better trained than Caitlin was," Jasmine said. "No offense to Caitlin. She was thrown into this business so all of a sudden, but like she says, she has her own witchy talents."

"No offense taken," Caitlin said, smiling.

Fiona saw Jasmine as a take-charge person who had goals in mind and accomplished them. Fiona couldn't even imagine how brave she had to be to confront and take down rogue vampires. That would be a scary business. Caitlin was more—sweet and cheerful and...human. Even though she was a vampire now like the rest. But she also had this fun witch's side to her that made her less human and more capable of handling trouble. Fiona was kind of like her in that she hadn't had the experience of fighting bad guys with her abilities. But her abilities weren't magical in the least. Well, except for the dream powers she might have, though she wasn't sure everyone knew what they were talking about.

"So what do you all think about the possibility of me having this dream persuasion power?" Fiona wanted to know if they thought she should get rid of it, or could she maybe use it for good? That's what she was thinking of. If she chose which way for a character to go in a book she was reading that had choices, she always chose the right path. Well, except when she wanted to see what would happen if she made wrong choices just for fun. She handed Stasio's phone back to him.

She had taken martial arts classes from the age of three on. In school, she had always stuck up for kids who couldn't or wouldn't defend themselves. She wasn't afraid of bullies, though she had to make sure she didn't look like one in return.

No one said anything. They probably didn't know what to think of her having such a power.

"Okay, so, Stasio, the historical genius…," she said.

Stasio smiled.

Fiona smiled and continued. "What have you learned about my dealing with the power? A way of ending the curse? Or a way to control it for the benefit of others, not using it for bad?"

Then Stasio sat up taller and finished his slice of pizza. He drank some of his soda and said, "You have to find your dream mate."

She raised her brows.

Stasio shrugged. "That's what the ancient book said. The one afflicted with the ability must find his or her dream mate and that will end the curse."

"There are others who have this ability?" Fiona was surprised. She had the notion she was the only one. That she was special. She felt deflated all at once.

"We've never known anybody that has that ability," Levka said, "but you and Arman have had the dreams connecting the two of you, right?"

She nodded.

"That's not to say he's your dream mate," Levka quickly said. "But that's what made us research your existence and learn all we could about you. That's how we learned you have this curse."

"Isn't it illegal for a vampire to turn a hunter?" Fiona asked, suddenly thinking that it should be if it wasn't already.

"Aye," Levka said. "But rogues will do whatever they want to gain any power they want. That's what makes them rogues and dangerous."

That's what Fiona was afraid of. "So about my question, do you think it would be better to end the curse or not?"

"It depends on the person who has the power," Levka said. "If you can control it and only use it to help others, then it would be a gift. If it becomes a tool to terrorize people, then it could be a curse."

"It *could* be," Fiona said.

"Right. Unless the people you are terrorizing are...," Levka said.

"Rogues." Now Fiona liked that idea.

Levka smiled.

"Like Tobias and Regina. Clarissa even. I mean, could I even slip into their dreams and give them nightmares?" Fiona couldn't even imagine being able to do it to just plain humans. Look at *her* thinking of people in that way when that's all she had ever been. Human, through and through. Or so she had thought. But to be able to control the powerful vampires' dreams? She didn't think she would be capable of that.

"If what is written is true, yes," Stasio said.

"Okay, so if I wanted to get rid of the curse, how would I go about it?" Fiona asked. If she had to die, she wasn't going for it. She liked the idea of having some special power all her own, but not if people wanted to use her for her abilities, or wanted her dead if she wouldn't go along with the plan.

They all looked at Arman to explain.

"It has something to do with us," Arman said. "You and I both have been sharing dreams."

She tilted her chin down and gave him a look. "You better

not say that you have to turn me into a vampire and that will get rid of the ability."

Arman smiled, and he had the most devilishly wicked smile of any guy she'd ever known. Instead of sending chills through her, his expression gave her a little thrill. But she did *not* want to be turned into a vampire. Drink blood? Yuck.

"We don't know," Arman said, losing the smile. "It's just that we are connected in some way and my dreams indicate I'm supposed to save you."

"How do you remember them? I have vague recollections of you, but I can't remember most of the details for the life of me when I wake up." Maybe he could remember his because of having a vampire condition.

"They wake me, and I write them down."

"Oh." So it wasn't something magical he could do. She was a little disappointed. "So tell me what all you can do as vampires so I know more what to expect."

"We can fly places, as you have learned. We can transport ourselves into places," Arman said.

"You have to be invited in, right?"

"No," Ruric said. "We have advanced beyond that."

Wow, so all the stuff she thought would help, wouldn't? "Holy ground is off limits, right? I could go to a church and be safe or throw holy water on a vampire and they would sizzle and die a grotesque death." There had to be some way to protect herself. What if these vampires decided she wasn't worth the trouble and left her to face her demons on her own? She had to be ready to fight Tobias and Regina without their help.

"No, and strings of garlic won't do anything either. Those are all myths. We regularly eat garlic in our meals," Jasmine said.

"Wooden stakes to the heart?" Fiona worried that even that was a myth.

Everyone smiled at her. Levka said, "Anything striking the

heart—a sword, wooden stake, an arrow—could kill vampires and humans alike. So yeah, it works."

"Or..." Ruric started to speak and then looked as though he thought better of what he was going to say.

"Or, what?" Fiona asked. There wasn't any time like the present to learn how she could take down a vampire.

"Cut off their head," Jasmine said. "But like with a stake or sword to the heart, cutting off the head for anyone is a permanent solution."

"Aww. Of course." Why didn't Fiona think of that? "What about drowning?"

"We can drown, just like anyone else," Arman said. "Being buried alive in soil?" He shook his head. "If the vampire is powerful enough, he'll make his way out of it."

"The sun!"

"On days where the sun is really intense, we burn badly. So we avoid going out or cover up well. But during the day if it's overcast? We don't have any issues," Stasio said.

"Yeah, I was worried about that," Caitlin said. "Not that I was into suntanning. I always just burned. But that I would have to live a life only at night? Or that the sun could make me disintegrate? That was not an appealing way to live."

"The only ones who disintegrate are the old ones," Arman said.

Fiona frowned. "Aren't you old ones?"

"Yeah. So if someone kills us, we would turn to ash," Arman said.

"But if you're more...uhm, newly turned like Caitlin?" Fiona hated to even bring it up, but she had to know how this all worked.

"She would look like a regular person if she died," Jasmine said.

"Okay, so let's say you protect me through the blood moon,

then what? They leave me alone? They can't steal my power? What?"

"Tobias wanted to turn you to gain your power, but he can't do it until the night of the blood moon," Arman said. "If he turned you, then you can't kill the one who makes you."

"Ohmigod, so you're like a puppet? Playing to their whim?"

"Essentially," Levka said.

Fiona looked at Caitlin.

Caitlin shrugged. "I would have died if Levka hadn't saved my life. I have no regrets. And he in no way controls me."

Levka gave Caitlin a smug smile.

"Not that he doesn't try sometimes." Caitlin gave him a hug and he kissed her back.

"It's truly a condition of the princes having been princes," Jasmine said, smiling at Stasio.

He pulled her onto his lap and kissed her. "I was just lucky I changed your mind about eliminating us."

"Ha! You left me no other alternative." Jasmine turned to Fiona. "I had to go on the run with them because of association. I had made the mistake of telling hunters that I was Stasio's girlfriend. I thought he was a vampire hunter like me. Not a rogue. The princes had tried to overthrow the ruling League in Wales. They lost the battle and were branded rogues."

Stasio smiled. "You know it all worked out for the best between us."

"It did. These guys get themselves into the worst binds and then miraculously get themselves out of them with a little help from friends, I might add," Jasmine said.

"Like with coming to my aid." Fiona had to give them credit for coming to help her out when they didn't even know her.

"Exactly," Ruric said. "Speaking of which, we need to head to Houston and get on our flight."

"Do we have any layovers? Or do we have to make any other

connections?" Fiona hoped not. She thought if they could get on the flight and be out of here, they would be safe. As long as Tobias and Regina didn't pick up their trail.

"It's a straight shot, no stops," Ruric said.

"Oh great." Fiona was so relieved.

"Let's go," Levka said, and they dumped their trash in the trash bins, then headed outside into the fresh air on the perfectly cloudy day. "We're going to get rain."

"Yeah," Jasmine said. "So let's hurry."

"Can rain hurt you?" Fiona figured that would be a disaster. What if they couldn't fly in rain?

Jasmine smiled. "No, but we'll all be soaked to the skin and that will make for an uncomfortable flight."

"Oh, true. How long is the flight?"

"Twelve hours," Ruric said.

That wasn't going to be fun.

They reached the terminal just as the rain let loose and everyone breathed a sigh of relief. Except for Stasio.

"What's wrong, Stasio?" Fiona asked, since no one seemed to notice he appeared anxious, not even his girlfriend.

"He doesn't like to fly," Jasmine said. "Not in a plane, anyway."

"That's awful." Especially since they had to fly so far to get to where they were going. "Then after we get to Scotland, what are we going to do?"

"We're going to a safe house," Arman said. "I'm sure that you'll enjoy it. It has an indoor swimming pool and a tennis court even."

"Wow. That sounds nice. Do you have any pictures of it?" Then Fiona realized she had his phone.

"No."

"What? Why not?"

"I never thought to take any pictures of it."

Fiona glanced at the others, but they just smiled at her and shook their heads. "Oh, it's a safe house."

"Right, so no posting about the place online."

With disappointment, Fiona realized she would never be able to get back to her social media online. Well, maybe only after she reached eighteen and got rid of the curse...or just managed to make it through the phase of the blood moon and Tobias and Regina no longer wanted to control her. Maybe then. Or not.

11

Arman hoped Fiona would be happy with them. Caitlin and Jasmine had fit right in with their little group of vampires who were always trying to get themselves out of one issue or another, but he wasn't sure how Fiona was feeling about all the changes in her life. He knew she'd been unhappy with Regina and Tobias and had wanted to leave that situation behind as soon as she could. But it didn't mean she would want to stay with them in Scotland. What if she wanted to meet other hunters like herself? Learn about their ways? Join a hunter family? Marry a hunter mate?

He wasn't ready to tell her what Stasio had shared with him earlier today after digging through more online archives. Something he'd discovered that Arman didn't think she was ready to learn about.

Stasio glanced back at him as they boarded the plane. Arman knew Stasio wanted him to tell Fiona what he had learned, but couldn't that wait until they reached the safehouse in Scotland? Arman didn't want to upset her. What if she decided to deplane while other passengers were still boarding?

Ruric was sitting in the aisle seat next to Arman, who was in the middle, and Fiona had the seat next to the window. Levka and Caitlin were sitting in the seats in front of them. Arman swore he always had to lead, even if he was in a seat on an airplane leading the way. Stasio and Jasmine were sitting in the seats across the aisle from Ruric, Arman, and Fiona.

If Ruric could have, he would have gotten them all first-class seats, but Levka had said not to bother because there were getting to be so many in their little vampire pack. He hadn't wanted them to cause an incident if they bumped all the first-class passengers suddenly. It was a good thing too, because two of the first-class passengers were vampires.

The man and woman were having an open telepathic conversation about seeing the sights in Edinburgh, most likely thinking, wrongly, that no one onboard could be vampires listening in. They looked to be about twenty-five, but who knew in vampire ages. The man and woman had looked similar, both redheads, freckled, about the same build—slender, tall. They were dressed in black jeans, white shirts, black leather jackets and black boots. Arman was certain they were related. If not brother and sister, close cousins possibly.

Arman really hoped that they wouldn't cause trouble for them.

Then the stewardess made the safety announcements and before long, they were in the air. Arman was so glad that Regina and Tobias hadn't discovered them before they left the States. Though Regina and Tobias might end up going to Wales to see if they returned there, or they could find someone else to go in their stead. He just hoped Regina and Tobias wouldn't learn about the coup in Scotland that Arman and his friends had been instrumental in and search for them there.

As soon as they were airborne, they settled back in their seats to make the most of the long flight. Stasio had been doing much better traveling by plane now that Jasmine was with him so Arman hoped it would help this time also.

The stewardesses started handing out drinks and once they both got a bottled water, Fiona said to Arman, "Okay, so what did you learn?"

"About what?"

She turned her head to look out the window.

He figured he was in the doghouse now. How would she have learned he knew something he didn't want to share with her just yet?

"Stasio learned something, glanced back at you, gave you a look that said he wanted you to tell me the truth about something he had learned, and you looked at me, so I know it was about me."

"Us," Arman said, figuring he couldn't get away with keeping secrets from her.

"Us? You mean with the whole lot of you?" Fiona asked.

"You and me. Us. If we left the pack, it would still have to do with you and me."

"Okay, what then?"

"I can help you with your ability."

She narrowed her eyes at him. "You want the power for yourself?"

"No, I'm just saying that because we're dream-connected, I can help you with it when you get the ability, I think. At least Stasio believes. Even though he found where someone had done it before and it had worked, it doesn't mean it would with us. We're not sure."

"Who did it before? Maybe we can talk to them and learn more about it and how it was done. Does the person with the ability use it and how? Did anyone come after them with the same dark interest and threaten to kill them if they didn't give into them? Are they still alive?"

This was just why Arman hadn't wanted to tell her about it on the plane. "Your father has the ability."

"What? No...no...no...no."

"We think that's why you have the ability."

"Were they hunters then?"

This got tricky. "They were."

"Were? Are they no longer alive?" Fiona's voice hitched.

"That...we don't know. Tobias...Tobias was after your dad for the same ability he wants from you. Your mother tried to kill Tobias to protect your father, but he—"

"Killed her?" Fiona sounded like she was ready to take on the vampire herself now.

"No. He turned her. She became a huntress turned vampire. Tobias thought he could control her. He believed he could make her hand over your father to him so he could turn him, but instead she turned Nathaniel herself."

"Wait, what? My parents are both vampires now? How could I be a huntress? Oh...oh, I got it. I was born before they were turned. They gave me up to the dysfunctional humans because the vampires were after my dad. My parents hadn't wanted them to know the baby—me—might have this ability too."

"That's what we figure. Your mother can't kill Tobias."

"Because he made her. But she turned my dad, why?"

"Because he could protect himself better. Tobias can't control him. Your dad can kill him if he gets the chance."

"What...what if Tobias wants me because he wants to draw them to him? To me? They would come to rescue me, and he would kill them."

"That's a good possibility. Or at least he could be after your father because Tobias has no control over him. And Tobias wouldn't want him interfering with his plans for you."

"Then we need to kill Tobias and end his reign of terror."

Arman sighed. "We're all in agreement but we have to teach you how to use a sword in a fight. Not just in demonstrations."

"I can't just kill anyone."

"No. But we'll all put you through your paces."

"Practice fighting. Okay, I like that idea. I don't have any sword with me. You don't either."

"No, but we have an armory filled with them back at the safe house."

"Oh, okay. Wow. I didn't know I had joined a militant group."

Arman smiled. Little did she know.

"Did my parents give me up because they thought they couldn't raise me since they were vampires, and I was still a hunter?"

"I doubt it. I'm sure it all had to do with wanting to protect you from Tobias, or other vampires with the same dark plan." Now for the really hard part. "If one of us turns you—"

Fiona looked cross with him and folded her arms. "Yeah?"

"Then you'll really be able to fight the vampires on more equal terms. Jasmine is a vampire who hunts rogues. Maybe you could join her on some hunts."

Fiona's brows rose. "You want her to turn me?"

"No, I'm just saying you might end up being a vampire huntress like her. Any one of us could turn you."

"Not Levka."

Arman smiled just a hint.

"He's too controlling, though Caitlin holds her own. I could see me butting heads with Levka and him trying to make me do things because he made me."

"He wouldn't. But Caitlin can't turn you either, because she doesn't want to turn anyone."

"I don't blame her. What about you? Would you have any qualms about it?"

"Hell, yeah. I mean, I would do it in a heartbeat—"

She reached over and felt his chest.

He smiled at her. "We still have beating hearts."

"So another misnomer."

"Exactly. We're not dead. We breathe, eat, and drink. We do just about everything that humans do but we have a need for extra blood, and no soaking up the sun on the beach, but that's not good for anyone either. Otherwise, we have a lot of powers that really help us out. Like night vision, for one. Our hearing is enhanced, but it's like that for hunters too. Anyway, as I was saying, I would do anything to protect you. That's why I left the safety of Scotland to rescue you."

She sighed. "But if you turned me, what do you get out of it?"

"A friend who lives a lot longer than a huntress."

"Unless a vampire or hunter ends me."

"We all have that problem. Even as a huntress you can be on someone's terminal list."

"How well I know."

Then the stewardesses handed out dinners and they both selected the chicken dish. Once they finished eating, they watched Stasio head back to the restroom.

"I'm okay," Stasio said when he caught their eye.

"Good," Arman said.

Stasio smiled. "Jasmine is good for me, especially when we travel by plane." Then he made his way to the restroom.

"I was going to see if I could help him if he tried to sleep after dinner." Fiona settled against her seat back, her airline pillow behind her head and the blanket over her lap.

"Can you do that now?" Arman thought maybe it had to happen the night of the blood moon and then she would have the ability.

"I can already give you pleasant dreams, it seems."

He smiled. "You sure can."

She laughed and closed her eyes. He settled back against his pillow and closed his eyes too. He really didn't think he could sleep. But the next think he knew, he was dreaming of her... Fiona Wilder, dreamer of dreams that made his own magical.

Fiona was racing after Arman on a beach. What the heck? He was supposed to be the one chasing after her and catching her! Hugging her. Kissing her.

Clouds covered the sky, making it the perfect day. Why wasn't he stopping to catch her in his arms? Why was he still running away? But then she caught up to him and grabbed him in her arms and hugged and kissed him. Just like he'd wanted to do with her. She was beautiful and for the moment all his.

F<small>IONA KNEW JUST</small> *what Arman thought she should be doing, but she wasn't going along with it. He wanted to chase her! So she changed the scenario. He tried to turn the dream around to the way he saw himself, the one who was coming for her, pursuing her, hunting her. But she wouldn't let him dream the scene in that way. In the end, the result was the same—them holding each other tight, kissing, enjoying the moment.*

She woke, feeling tired, but as soon as she woke, she remembered her dream and smiled. She liked the way she had changed it. Though it didn't mean Arman saw the dream in the same way if he even dreamed it. She might have dreamed it all on her own. She leaned over and snuggled against him. And then he was wrapping his arms around her and smiling.

"Did you dream of me?" he asked.

"Oh, yeah, I was chasing you."

"I was supposed to be chasing you," he said.

"I didn't want it that way."

He frowned at her. "You did not change my dream scenario."

"If we had the same dream and I wanted it to go one way and

you wanted it to go the other, I can make it happen my way. I think. I...I didn't realize I could do that. But, ohmigod, I already have the power. The ability. Maybe."

"With me."

"Yeah, maybe just with you. I love it."

He laughed. "You are in charge of me during our dreams."

"That works for me."

He laughed again. "The end result was just what I wanted."

"Yeah, see? Next time, I'll let you chase me."

He smiled and kissed her. "You've got it. What about nightmares?"

"Do you want me to give you a nightmare?"

He shook his head. "Not really, but I wonder if you can give anyone one."

"Hmm, I wonder if I can try giving the others a good dream first? Just to see if I can do it with anyone other than you."

Arman glanced over at Stasio and whispered to Fiona, "Stasio is asleep. Try it on him."

"Don't you think I should ask him first?"

Arman smiled. "Nah. He's a good sport."

"Alright, but if he gets mad about it, I'm telling him that you encouraged me to do it."

Arman chuckled. "Go for it."

She sighed and closed her eyes, but she couldn't fall asleep. Yet she attempted to connect with Stasio and see his dreams if he was having any. She didn't know how to do this. She tried and tried to break into his dreamlike state, but maybe he wasn't dreaming. Or maybe she had to be sleeping. Though she couldn't imagine bonding with anyone else like she could connect with Arman. She was resting her head against Arman's shoulder still, feeling relaxed, the sound of the airplane's engines droning on in the background.

She let out her breath and figured she couldn't do this, but as soon as she let go, she felt connected to Stasio in his dreamlike state.

Stasio was caught up in a nightmare, fighting a vampire, both of them armed with swords and she turned the other vampire's sword into a funnel of pink cotton candy. Immediately, both Stasio and the other vampire stopped their fight and were staring at the cotton candy. Did she do that?

The other vampire dropped the paper cone of cotton candy and turned and vanished. Stasio looked dumbfounded, but then he saw Jasmine coming to his rescue and he swept her up in his arms and they kissed. Time for Fiona to remove herself from the equation. She felt joy and relief that she could change a possible nightmare to a happier dream for her friends.

Then she opened her eyes and saw that Arman was watching a movie. She turned his phone on and looked through the photos on his camera. There were none but the ones she'd taken at Moody Gardens.

As soon as he realized she was awake, he pulled her close. She loved that he wanted to be intimate with her no matter what he was doing at the time. Watching the movie didn't seem to be as important to him.

"You took some great photos," he said.

She smiled at him. "Thanks. You don't have any photos of your own on here."

Arman smiled at her, looking more than amused. "No. What were you trying to find out?"

"If you had some pictures of some cute girlfriends."

He laughed. "I told you I didn't." He turned off the movie.

"You did tell me that. And I did it!"

"What? You got into Stasio's dream?"

She told Arman what had happened concerning the rogue vampire's sword turning into a cone of cotton candy. Arman laughed out loud. She loved that he could see the humor in situations.

"I couldn't believe I could turn a sword into a cone of cotton candy. I wish I could do it for real during a deadly fight."

"Now that would come in handy," Arman said. "Can you try it with one of our other friends?"

She was still just trying to find her way through all this. "Levka," she said.

"You like to tread dangerously."

She laughed. "I'm going to imagine he's sleeping and see if he's dreaming. I didn't have to fall asleep to enter Stasio's dream."

"That's incredible."

"Yeah, I was really surprised. I didn't think I could do that." Then she rested her head against Arman's shoulder and closed her eyes again. She concentrated on trying to connect with Levka with no luck at all. He might just be watching a movie, not asleep and dreaming about anything. She wondered really how useful her ability could be. If the only way to use it was when someone was dreaming, how would she even know that? She figured she had just gotten lucky with Stasio.

She would try each of her new friends. But she couldn't find any way to connect with their dreams. Then she thought she needed to wait until the lights were turned off for the red eye flight. At some point, maybe everyone would be asleep. She sighed and sat up in her seat.

"No luck?" Arman asked her.

"No. I'll have to wait until they turn out the overhead lights and everyone settles down to sleep."

Arman got up from his seat and visited with his friends for a moment. She hoped he wasn't telling them about what she did to Stasio and how she was trying to get into the others' dreams also, but then he returned to his seat.

"I didn't tell them anything about what you're doing or attempting to do. Everyone is watching different movies, so I was asking them what they thought of them."

She smiled. "Good. I want them to be unaware of what I plan to do, or they might be able to stop me in their dream. I'm not sure how this works. I might need to practice at it. But if they're all watching movies, that's the reason I couldn't connect with their dreams."

"Right. None of them are asleep yet. That's what I was checking out. Only Stasio was for a while."

Then she and Arman watched a movie together for an hour and a half until it was getting late, and they turned it off and snuggled against each other to sleep.

"Remember," he said, "I get to chase you this time."

She chuckled. "I need to train myself on how to do this, so we'll see." She figured she had to try and control the situation in the dream as much as possible. Then she frowned at him. "You don't think I would have more control over it if I were one of you, do you?"

"I'm not sure. But Tobias planned to turn your father, so it can't lessen the effects of the ability if you're one of us or Tobias wouldn't have planned on changing him. Mostly, we were just thinking you would have better protection against a vampire, being able to move more quickly, vanish, fly, etcetera, to keep out of the vampire's reach. Especially until you're able to learn how to fight them well. As a huntress, you'll be just as strong, but you can't vanish or take flying leaps to get out of the path of a vampire."

"Right, but no matter what, I won't be as capable of fighting, not until I've trained."

"True, but you can hold a sword. Caitlin even had trouble with that. She had to rely on her witch's skills more."

"You said my father's name was Nathaniel. What is my mother's name?"

"Bethany."

"And their last names?"

"Fairhaven. They were born in San Antonio, Texas and lived in Dallas, Texas for years."

"Where was I born?"

"San Antonio."

"So I'm really Fiona Fairhaven from San Antonio." She was going to have to get used to that. But she liked it. It suited her. But then she wondered... "Is my first name really Fiona?"

"Yeah, it is."

She breathed a sigh of relief. She was glad something was the same in her life.

12

Arman was sure ready to share a dream with Fiona again. He didn't even mind if she took charge if they had the same result. Though kissing her for real appealed even more. But when he tried to sleep, he found he couldn't. She seemed to be sleeping, and he was glad he had told her what Stasio had learned about her family and that she hadn't had a meltdown. Instead, she appeared to be eager to learn what she could about her powers and how she could really use them. Hopefully for good. And he hoped she would like to keep her abilities. Stasio hadn't learned if she could actually get rid of the curse.

Both Stasio and Ruric were using their skills to try and locate her parents in the meantime, and they hoped they would discover where they were and even more, that they would want to rejoin their daughter. Which made him wonder if they would even be happy that she was with a pack of vampires—helping her, sure, but would they prefer her to be with hunters? Finding a hunter mate?

Then he wondered what the deal was with Fiona's father.

Why was it that Tobias had to turn Fiona into a vampire the night of the blood moon when she turned eighteen, but her father and her mother had already been together? So wouldn't they have been older? Unless they hadn't turned eighteen yet. Or maybe something about Fiona made her different from her father. Arman couldn't quit thinking about it. Now he really couldn't get to sleep.

Fiona had curled up against the window and Ruric was zonked out. Stasio and Jasmine were cuddled together, their eyes closed, and he assumed they were sleeping. He didn't want to disturb Ruric by leaving his seat to see if Levka and Caitlin were asleep or not. But everyone seemed to be sleeping on the plane for the most part. He saw a couple of overhead lights on where people were reading books though.

Stasio didn't get as annoyed with anyone if they woke him up while he was sleeping like Levka did, so Arman asked him telepathically, *"Hey, Stasio. About your research, was Nathaniel Fairhaven eighteen during the blood moon when Tobias wanted to turn him and control his powers?"*

There was no response.

"Stasio?" Arman hated it when he couldn't get an answer to some question that was gnawing at his brain.

FIONA HAD PLANNED to sleep and enter someone's dream, but when she was dreaming, she wasn't with any of the vampires, just by herself, having a bizarre dream about babysitting a baby and wanting to wash it in the ocean, because everyone else was wading in the ocean. And they were waiting for her to take the baby in. But there was no beach. It was all boulders and so she was afraid she would slip off a slick boulder that was under water and the baby would be dunked. Then she began worrying that the ocean wasn't clean enough. What was that all about?

Who would ever think of washing a baby in saltwater? She woke herself from the dream and pondered it, but none of it made any sense. She figured it was just one of those weird nonsense dreams she often had. She glanced at Arman, and he smiled at her. Poor guy. It appeared he hadn't been able to sleep.

She snuggled up against him. "No luck on sleeping?"

"No. Any luck with changing anyone's dreams?"

"No. I didn't see anyone's dreams at all. They might have been in REM sleep. I really don't know how it all works. It appears everyone's asleep though," Fiona said.

"Yeah. I had a thought."

"Don't tell me. You wondered why Tobias was after my father when the magic time for me is eighteen and during the blood moon."

"Yeah, exactly. I tried to ask Stasio telepathically, but he's dead to the world. Unless he was ignoring me. But you might be right. Maybe for you it's eighteen. Maybe for your father, it was a different age and perhaps not even during the blood moon. Maybe during the wolf's moon. Or at some other particular time? Who knows? We just need to keep looking into it."

"And find my parents."

"Yeah, that goes without saying. Though—"

"They might not like that I'm hanging out with a bunch of nice rogue vampires."

Arman smiled. "You could say that. Though they're vampires now too. But they might want you to be with hunters like they had been."

"You accept me. You and your friends. Would hunters accept me if they knew I had parents who had been turned? I want to reconnect with my parents, so it's not like I would want to hide what they are from others."

"I'm sure some will accept you for who you are, and others won't. You know how it is."

"Oh, yeah. Even in school, it was definitely like that without even putting the hunter/vampire stigma to the test. I wonder why my parents wouldn't have given me to a hunter family."

"Maybe for the same reason they didn't want to keep you with them. That they were afraid that's the first place Tobias would look," Arman said.

"Or"—Fiona had to look at this realistically—"it's possible that other hunters didn't want the trouble. I mean, when you really think of it, that could put them more at risk too. Whereas finding a human family who needed money, they could more easily be bought off, don't you think?"

"A money trail," Arman said, snapping his fingers. "Unless your parents gave them a lumpsum payment."

"Or just used their vampire persuasion to make them believe I was their child."

"Oh." Arman looked defeated in that moment. "I keep forgetting that your parents would have been vampires by the time they had to find a new home for you. They definitely could have done that. But still, if they did pay them, it might have been in installments to make sure you were fed and clothed properly. Or your foster parents might have spent the whole amount on themselves. Do you remember your foster parents ever talking about the money they were getting for you?"

"Uhm, I remember them arguing about money. But I thought it was just that they weren't making enough. They were really frugal, but Dad spent so much on his alcohol or at pubs that the money might have been tight because of that. My brother and I did get gifts from an aunt and uncle who sent them at Christmas and for our birthdays. I tried to learn who they were, but they were just listed as Uncle Nat and Aunt Bea. My foster mom and dad never mentioned who they were or whose side of the family they were related to by blood. I never really thought to ask. For whatever reason, we always assumed they were on my mother's side of the family."

"It could have been a way for your biological parents to keep a connection with you if the gifts were from them and as a reminder, if they were paying your foster parents, to keep up the charade and spend the money on you that they were sending for your upkeep."

Fiona could understand that but what about her brother? "But they sent the gifts to my brother also. They were expensive gifts too. Updated computers every year. New cell phones every year. They gave my brother a car before he went to college, and when I turned seventeen, they gave me one too before my parents' untimely deaths, but Regina sold it, saying it would have cost too much to drive it all the way to Oregon."

"To make it seem more like they were truly your aunt and uncle, they would have needed to send gifts to both of you."

"Then if that's the case, wouldn't they have been monitoring what had happened to me after my foster parents died? They must have known that Regina took me to Oregon. Why didn't they come to rescue me?"

"What if your father still has the gift of dreams? What if he connected with me in some way to come and help you out? Maybe it was the both of you who encouraged me to come? The man was blond-haired who had visited me."

"Oh, wow. A blond-haired man also came to see me. But why wouldn't he have physically come for me?"

"It's possible that by the time your mother and father learned your foster parents had died it was too late. And then when Regina took you in, she was surrounded by her own pack of vampires. That would have been too many vampires for them to deal with if your parents aren't in a pack of their own."

"Then why would my father make a connection with you?" Fiona didn't think it made any sense.

"What if you and I had this connection, for whatever reason, and your father could listen in on your dreams? Then he interceded on your behalf to me in a dream way to go to your aid. Maybe he and your mother researched who I was and learned that my friends and I had successfully removed the vampires who were in control of the League of Vampires in Scotland, no easy task, and thought we might be up to the mission."

"Hmm."

"It couldn't be random," Ruric said, his eyes still closed.

Fiona and Arman smiled at him.

Had Ruric been listening to their conversation the whole time?

"I think you hit on something with the idea that you and Fiona were dreaming about each other, and her father joined in on the dream and then learned who Arman was. But also since we travel together, he would have learned who all of us are and realized we might be able to help you out," Ruric said.

"But he has to realize we are considered rogues, by some leagues," Arman said. "I still don't know why you and I connected."

"Because we were at the Dallas mall, and I spilled a soda on you earlier? What if that wasn't by accident? Then again, maybe it was just meant to be. I felt lost when my foster parents died and then there you were in my dreams, telling me I was important, loved, special. You don't know how much I needed to hear that. And then when I saw you at the Halloween party, I couldn't believe it was you. It couldn't have been. You were just a dream to me. A figment of my imagination. Not a real person. Yet once I saw you, I thought of you being at the Dallas mall and how I was instantly drawn to you, attracted to you, and that had never happened to me before."

"I felt the same way about you. But I thought I could control you with my vampiric gaze, bring you with me and protect you and I wasn't able to. I knew for certain that you weren't just a human girl I was supposed to save."

Ruric started to snore. Arman and Fiona smiled.

"Did that bother you that I wasn't a human who could easily be persuaded to do as you commanded?" Fiona asked.

Arman sighed and then smiled. "It meant I had to work harder at it, do more research, find out what we needed to do to keep you safe, which was certainly worth it. No, it didn't bother me that you were a huntress. What bothered me was that you didn't know it. You could have been a prime candidate for a rogue vampire to eliminate you, especially since you had no other hunters to help you."

"Like Tobias."

"Right. Like him and Regina."

"But how did you and I...connect in dreams later? Did it really have to do with us running into each other at the mall? That's what I don't understand."

"Fate." He said it so seriously that she smiled at him. "It's true. How else would you explain it?"

"Okay, I'll buy it, since we have no other idea of how it happened. Oh, I wanted to ask you about the couple in the first-class seats on the plane who were talking telepathically to each other. Were they vampires?"

"Or they could be hunters who have the ability—which is rare. I've only heard of one like that. But I have to tell you that Caitlin had the ability also. Maybe because she was also a witch."

Fiona frowned at Arman. "What if they work for Regina and Tobias? Or are friends of theirs and they even know who we are?"

"Hopefully they aren't. They could try to contact some other vampires who might be friends of theirs in Scotland to come to their aid against us. But I'm hoping that's not the case. They didn't seem to really take notice of us when we walked past them. Though I had glanced at them for a split second, they didn't react. Many passengers glance at who is in the various seats, so that they would not think anything was suspicious about that."

"True. Uhm, did you really want to dance with me at the Halloween dance?"

"You bet."

"And you shoved Toga Guy halfway across the gym floor with your vampiric strength? Here I thought you might be kind of a geek. Though a really awesome looking geek."

He smiled at her. "Thanks. I didn't want to scare you, but I did want to get you away from there and to the house we had rented so we could talk to you about what was going on. Dancing with you totally appealed."

"Even though I'm a hunter."

"I never really gave it a thought."

"It didn't matter how I was dressed for the affair?" She couldn't imagine that someone dressed in a tux would have been interested in dancing with someone who was dressed to fight—martial arts style.

"Are you kidding? The first thought I had was I was glad you weren't wearing tons of fake blood like the others at the dance, and the second thought I had was I was glad that you probably knew some lethal moves of your own and that they could come in handy in our line of work."

"I couldn't believe so many of the kids were dressed as zombies. Nor could I believe that you were…are a vampire for real."

"Or that you're a huntress from a long line of hunters."

"Right. Okay, I'm going to try and go to sleep again," she said.

"Good," Ruric said.

Fiona and Arman chuckled. Then the two of them tried to sleep.

Before they knew it, the lights were coming on in the cabin, and the stewardesses were bringing them breakfast. Where did the time go? Fiona really hadn't thought she would sleep. She sure thought she would have dreamed. Unless... unless she had forgotten them upon waking, which was what often happened.

"Did you dream about me?" she asked Arman.

"No. I was so tired, I think I just slept the night through, or I just don't remember any dream once I woke."

"I dreamed of Fiona's friend running into me with her car," Ruric said, sitting up and eating his breakfast.

"Oh, I'm so sorry about that." Fiona still felt badly about it, though she was really glad they hadn't hurt him. She wished she could have slipped into his dreams and given him more pleasant ones.

"But then something strange happened." Ruric drank some of his orange juice. "I was suddenly seeing the car accident in a whole different perspective. Instead of a car running me down, Fiona knocked me down with a big pillow."

Arman and Fiona just stared at him. "No, you did not see that." She drank her water.

"Yeah. I swear I did. One minute, I was being hit by the car, and the next, the vehicle is there, headlights shining in my eyes, and Fiona checks me to see how injured I was. But then the whole scenario changed like it rewound itself and instead of the car striking me, Fiona socks me with a big red pillow."

"The color of Emma's car," Fiona said. "It's like you mixed up a red pillow, something soft, for the car that hit you."

"The pillow wasn't all that soft when you used it on me. I mean, the way you slugged me with it, you have quite a swing,"

Ruric said. "So you visited my dreams and took away my nightmare, kind of?"

"I...I don't remember dreaming about that. You must have just dreamed it on your own." Fiona wondered if she would get more control over this dream business when she was eighteen, during the blood moon.

"Maybe you just don't remember it," Arman said. "You told me you often don't recall your dreams."

"True." She sure wished she could remember them better.

Then Caitlin got out of her seat and stopped by their row. "Fiona, thanks for changing my nightmare into something more pleasant."

"What...what were you dreaming of?" Fiona was totally puzzled by all this. How could she visit two people's dreams, if she had, and change nightmares into something easier to cope with and not even realize she'd done it?

"I was dreaming of sharks swimming around me in the ocean while Levka was trying to keep me safe," Caitlin said. "I still have that nightmare from time to time after that had happened for real. The next thing I knew, Levka and I were floating in a nice warm swimming pool, and the only shark in the pool was a big float. What a relief, so thanks. Got to run to the little girl's room."

Arman and Ruric looked at Fiona. She lifted a shoulder. "I don't remember anything about dreaming anything. Truly."

Stasio finished his eggs. "You turned an enemy's sword into a funnel of cotton candy."

"What color?" Jasmine asked, then bit into her toast.

"Pink," Fiona said.

"So you remember Stasio's dream?" Jasmine asked.

"I visited it last night." Fiona couldn't understand how she remembered that dream and not the others. Then again, *she* hadn't been asleep at the time.

"Well, I dreamed a vampire hunter was about to take me down for joining up with the rest of the pack. In the real case, hunters came to my rescue. But in my dream, you came and fought with the vampire hunter using your martial arts skills and sent his sword flying. He bared his teeth at you, and you bared yours right back at him," Jasmine said.

"Vampire teeth? You don't have premonitions, do you?" If Jasmine did, would that mean someone would turn Fiona?

"No, this was just a dream I had," Jasmine said.

"Oh." Fiona guessed Stasio hadn't had any other dreams, or he would have mentioned them to her.

Levka got out of his seat, and he glanced in her direction, but he didn't tell her that he'd had any dream that she was instrumental in. Instead, he headed back to the bathroom. Was he afraid to tell her she had helped him with his dream also? She could imagine him acting as though he was invincible, and no one had to assist him with anything, especially his dreams. But maybe he didn't want to even share he had them, or that he could have nightmares.

"You said you were Welsh princes. Did you have a castle?" Fiona asked.

"Each of us did, but they were taken away from us," Arman said. "Someday, I'll take you to see mine."

"That's such a shame, but I would love to see the castle."

"It's a hotel now, so we can even stay there."

"As long as no one who is hunting rogue vampires learns you are there," Ruric said.

"There is that," Arman agreed.

Caitlin came back by their row. "You are going to love your new home."

"I'm sure I will." At least Fiona sure hoped so. The thing about leaving a bad home, she figured anything else had to be better.

Then Levka returned and Caitlin took her seat.

"Did I visit your dreams?" Fiona wasn't afraid to ask him, and she suspected everyone was waiting for her to ask the question.

Levka only gave her a dark smirk and then retook his seat.

"I would take that as a yes," Ruric said.

"For sure," Arman agreed.

Now Fiona was dying to know exactly what part she had played in Levka's dream. Maybe she had given him a nightmare, instead of a pleasant dream. He could have really been enjoying his dream until she came along. She sighed. She needed to learn how to control the dream business whenever she used it in any scenario.

Then they finally landed and deboarded the plane. She was looking around for the vampires who had been on the flight and Arman reached down and squeezed her hand. "I don't see them, do you?"

"No." She was surprised he was looking for them too. But with all the trouble he'd been in, she guessed she could understand that he would be just as wary as she was.

"Do you see them?" Levka asked telepathically and everyone responded, *"No."*

She was glad that everyone was treating them as suspicious, just in case. But they had been sitting in first class and got off the plane first so Fiona and her companions hadn't had any way of getting after them any quicker than... Fiona looked around. Where was Caitlin?

Levka said to them, *"Caitlin was invisible when we landed and was waiting for the vampires to get off the plane. But I don't see her anywhere and she can't telepathically communicate with just us, so she has to be silent."* Levka sounded worried that he'd lost her.

"Should we spread out?" Arman asked.

"In twos. I don't want us all to be separated and lose more of us."

Levka glanced at Fiona as if he was even more worried about her.

Arman said to Fiona, "Do you want to stick with me?"

"Yeah, sure."

Ruric and Levka stayed together and Jasmine and Stasio began searching the airport too.

13

While searching for Caitlin at the airport, Fiona was really worried about her because she was a newly turned vampire and couldn't fight the way the others could. Though if she remained invisible, wouldn't she be safe? But the fact that Caitlin couldn't send anyone telepathic messages meant only for them didn't help the situation. Fiona was also concerned that something could have happened to her and it would all be Fiona's fault because she was certain it would have had all to do with her.

"Caitlin, are you safe? Where are you?" Fiona assumed Levka would have already asked her that, but Caitlin hadn't answered him. *"This is Fiona."* She thought she better add that in case Caitlin didn't recognize her voice.

But then she remembered that Caitlin couldn't respond telepathically to her, or she would alert any vampire in the building that she was there, telling them where she was.

"We need to go to baggage claim in case the vampires who were in first-class seating are picking up their luggage," Fiona said.

"Okay, let's go that way. They might be going to get transportation, a rental car, or a shuttle to a parking lot also," Arman said.

Levka said, *"Ruric and I are going to the shuttles and taxis."*

"We're going to baggage claim," Fiona said.

"We'll check out the restrooms," Jasmine said. *"That's the first place I go after getting off the plane."*

"Good idea," Arman said.

On the way past the restrooms, Arman and Fiona didn't see Caitlin. Jasmine went inside the women's restroom and Stasio headed into the men's room, but there were others too, so the vampire couple might have even gone down to the restrooms near the baggage claim or even to the restrooms near where the shuttles were.

Fiona and Arman headed down the escalator to the baggage claim and when they got there, they saw people standing around at the conveyer belts from different flights, waiting for their luggage to be offloaded from the planes.

"There!" Fiona saw both the male and female vampires. But no sign of Caitlin. Then she remembered Caitlin had been invisible when she left the plane.

"I'll tell the others the vampires are here," Arman said to Fiona. *"And hope that Caitlin is here."*

Then someone hugged Fiona but no one was there. She nearly screamed out in fright. "Is it you, Caitlin?" She whispered the words so no one else would hear.

Caitlin laughed and Fiona smiled. Now that was a cool, *really super cool* ability to have. Fiona wished she could do that. She didn't think the dream stuff was half as worthwhile to have. Unless there was something more to it.

Though it was startling to have an invisible person grab Fiona. But she was thrilled that Caitlin was fine, and she immediately telepathically transmitted to everyone, *"Caitlin is standing next to me at the baggage claim."*

Everyone else was coming down the stairs. They didn't need

to collect baggage and Levka said to everyone, *"Let's go. We have our ride."*

Now that was nice. A limousine maybe. Fiona laughed at herself. *As if.*

Then they went outside and Levka was hugging a visible Caitlin and kissing her. Fiona smiled. She was glad Caitlin was safe and the couple was back together again.

What she couldn't believe was Levka was standing next to a black limousine, and it *was* their ride.

They climbed into it. The black-haired chauffeur was about to shut the door when the two vampires who had been on the plane, their bags in hand, tried to get into the limo.

"Private conveyance, ma'am, sir," the chauffeur said, holding his hand out to stop them.

"They're going to want us with them," the man said.

"Who are you?" Levka asked.

"Someone you want on your side."

"Alright, we'll bite. Get in."

"Is that a good idea?" Arman looked like he was worried about Fiona, and she appreciated his concern.

"Yeah," Levka said. *"I've called for reinforcements just in case."*

Fiona couldn't believe how organized the pack of vampires were. She was really enjoying getting to know them and wow, a limousine service? This was out of this world.

She still didn't trust the new vampire couple in the limousine though. As soon as the chauffer started to leave the airport, Levka asked, "Do you know who we are?"

"Yeah. The four of you are the vampire princes of Wales. Caitlin is a witch. Jasmine is a vampire hunter." The guy shook his head. "You have formed a strange little group of vampires. And now you have Fiona in your pack who is a huntress, and she's wanted by some powerful vampires."

"So what we need to know is who the two of you are," Levka said. "And how you know all about us."

"I'm Shelly and this is my brother, Michail," the woman said.

"How do you know about Fiona?" Arman asked.

"We know Regina and Tobias. We're not friends of theirs but we learned they had taken Fiona hostage even though she didn't know that she was their hostage," Shelly said. "And that Fiona had some ability that they wanted to control. We just learned about the curse and the blood moon."

"Why didn't you come to my aid then?" Fiona asked, sounding suspicious, just like Arman felt about them and their motives.

Michail nodded. "By the time we learned what was going on with you and where you were located, Arman was trying to grab Fiona at her high school Halloween dance. We followed her home, but Tobias was watching out the window and we knew with just the two of us, we couldn't fight him. We couldn't believe you grabbed her at the high school the next day. We never thought all of you would pretend to be high school students. It was a brilliant move, really."

No one in their little pack looked like they were buying the whole scenario, but they were politely listening.

"And you're here now, why?" Ruric asked.

"To help you," Michail said.

"Help us," Stasio said.

"Yeah. I know you probably don't feel you can trust us, but we saved Fiona's brother. We knew he wasn't Fiona's blood relation, but we also knew that Regina and Tobias would want to eliminate him too. They planned to kill everyone in the family so that they would be able to convince Fiona that she had no one in the world who was left that she could trust," Shelly said.

"Where is Justin?" Fiona asked, sounding desperate to believe them.

Arman couldn't believe these two vampires were here, coming to aid them, so what exactly was their deal? Did they have an agenda? Everyone usually had an agenda.

"Justin is safe here in Scotland, actually," Michail said. "He's human, so he's a lot more vulnerable to suggestion than...say... you are. We told him he was to go to Scotland because he won a lot of money and was staying at a Scottish estate. Yours, in fact. We made him forget he was going to college, or he might have resisted the idea."

"He's in Scotland?" Fiona asked, sounding shocked.

"Yes. We knew Levka and his team of vampires would take you there," Shelly said. "Which is why we headed for Scotland after we learned the rest of you had taken Fiona from the high school. Of course, we thought you might go to Dallas to find your brother, or more news of him so we made a detour there."

"Wait, I saw the news about it. Levka and the others did too. He was dead, according to the papers and Regina," Fiona said.

"Right. Like you can trust anything Regina or Tobias say. No, Justin isn't dead. We actually made it look that way so that Regina and Tobias wouldn't actually be able to terminate him. Would you like to talk to him?" Shelly handed a cell phone to Fiona.

She hesitated to take it. Then she took a deep breath, took it, and called her brother's number.

"Hello?" Justin asked.

"Ohmigod, Justin, is that really you?"

"Fiona?"

"Yes. Are you in Scotland?"

"Yeah. I...uhm, am at some swanky castle-like estate. It's amazing. I won a trip here and ten-thousand dollars."

"Where is he?" Fiona asked Shelly.

"Like Michail said, he's at the estate that Levka and the rest of them call home. We dropped him off there to keep him safe, then returned to the States to rescue you before the blood moon," Shelly said.

"Look, we learned who you were and what you've done in Scotland," Michail said to Levka and the others. "We found the estate you had taken over. We knew you all had been trying to right some wrongs and we felt you would be good for Fiona. And that's why we took Justin there. Now, it's up to Fiona, but we think it would be safer for Justin if he was turned."

Fiona's mouth dropped open. "No."

Michail shrugged. "You and he would both be safer against the threat. It won't take Regina and Tobias long to learn where you've been taken to, and they'll bring reinforcements. We had considered taking Justin somewhere else where he wouldn't be around you and probably safer in a way. But we also knew you would want to see him. And he possibly could be safer with your friends."

"Justin, are you still there?" Fiona asked.

"Yeah. Are you close by?" Justin asked.

"We're, I mean, I'm coming to see you."

"Okay, that's great. They have a swimming pool and everything."

"Wonderful. I'll see you in…" Fiona glanced at Arman.

"Two hours."

"Two hours," Fiona said to her brother.

"Super. I'll see you then."

She ended the call and handed the phone back to Shelly. "Do you know anything about my parents and where they might be?"

"Oh, they sent us," Michail said.

"What? Why didn't you say that first?" Fiona asked.

Arman thought she didn't believe them. He had a hard time

believing it too. As soon as Shelly and Michail tried to gain entrance into the limo, that was the first thing they should have mentioned.

"There's just so much to tell before Levka and his friends decided we were the enemy and tried to eliminate us," Shelly said. "We took an awful risk moving your brother from his dorm when Regina and Tobias intended to eliminate him. We had to make it look like he had died. We took just as much of a risk getting into the limo with all of you. We talked openly on the plane telepathically so you would hear us. Do you think we were just being careless? We did it on purpose to let you know we were there. We took first class seats so that if any of Tobias or Regina's minions had followed you, we would have dealt with them."

Now Arman was surprised to hear that.

"Where are my parents?" Fiona asked.

"We were good friends of theirs for years."

"Were you hunters first too?" Fiona asked.

"No. We got to know them after they had been turned. We'd known Tobias and Regina back then, and we helped your parents to find human parents who could raise you before Tobias and Regina learned you even existed. But the problem was that Regina and Tobias found out about you just a few weeks before your foster parents' car accident."

"Did you know my foster dad was an alcoholic and my mother was an enabler?" Fiona asked, sounded irritated to the core.

"No. Your parents had tried to find hunter parents to take you in, hunters who had been friends of theirs for years, but no one would do it for them even though you were a huntress. So your mother and father had to quickly find human parents before Tobias and Regina learned of you. Your parents found a young couple with a son that needed the money, and they made arrangements to pay them monthly allotments to take care of both you and their son so that it appeared you were both their children," Shelly said.

"Where are my parents now?" Fiona asked.

Michail said, "They are coming to Scotland. They have kept in touch with us and we've let them know what has happened in the last several weeks, but they have been out of the country for years."

"But why not get in touch with me?" Fiona asked.

"Being what we are and what you are, they felt they needed to see you in person to explain everything or you might not believe them," Shelly asked.

"Do you know anything about the curse I have?" Fiona asked.

"It's not a curse," Shelly said. "It's a beautiful ability. No, we don't know that much about it, but your dad does, and he plans to explain it all to you. That's what he says it is. Something that is wondrous, not a curse."

"Do you know if her parents want her to be a vampire or remain a hunter?" Arman realized just how much he didn't want to lose her if she decided to continue to be a huntress.

"That's totally up to Fiona," Michail said. "Your parents will talk to you about it though, Fiona."

"We are in agreement that you would be safer, Fiona, to have our abilities. Our kind can be ruthless, and you haven't been trained as a hunter. But ultimately, it's your choice," Shelly said.

"Does my brother know that you are vampires?" Fiona asked.

"No. You are a huntress, and the vampires couldn't control you, so no one could wipe your thoughts and tell you what they wanted you to believe. With a human, it's easy to do. He has no idea about what we are. We're just friends of your family and trying to make sure he has a good time in Scotland. It's up to you if you want to tell him what all of us are, you included," Shelly said.

"When are my parents coming to Scotland?" Fiona asked.

Arman realized she didn't even know them, but maybe through her dreams she might have had with her father, she would feel some connection when she was reunited with him. Arman just hoped her father wouldn't want to send her away to be with other hunters once the blood moon passed.

"They didn't tell us exactly when they would arrive, but they said they were on their way," Shelly said.

"I guess *you* couldn't have taken me in when I was a baby," Fiona said.

"We have always been vampires. We didn't know anything about raising a hunter child. Besides, we didn't learn about their circumstances until you were already placed with your foster parents," Michail said.

Wait. Didn't they say they had helped her parents find humans to raise Fiona?

14

Fiona couldn't believe that these vampires knew her own parents, or that her brother was still alive. She wanted to shout for joy. But she wanted to see her brother first, to know he really was safe. And her parents? That was going to be awkward. She didn't really know them. Her mother not at all. Her dad only through dreams, if indeed the blond-haired guy *was* her dad.

"Do you still have visions of me and the future?" Fiona asked Arman.

"Not once you were with me. I've never had visions before that."

"We...we met before. When I spilled my soda all over you."

Arman smiled. "I figured you were just trying to meet me in a different kind of way."

Fiona laughed. "Right. If I had known you were a vampire, I probably would have run the other way."

Arman sighed. "I'm one of the good guys."

"I had never known a vampire before."

He raised his brows.

"Well, I hadn't known Regina and Tobias or Clarissa were

vampires. I might have even met others in passing that I didn't realize were vampires either. If most vampires telepathically communicate with each other, they must do it with each other and no one else can listen in."

"That's a good bet," Levka said. "We never know who could hear us."

"Like with us," Michail said. "Which was done on purpose to clue you in."

"Do you have pictures of my parents?" Fiona asked Michail and his sister, Shelly.

"Uh, no. Sorry," Michail said.

Fiona thought then she would be able to connect the man in her visions with her father. She was disappointed that she couldn't. She couldn't wait until she could see her real parents and hoped they could become a family. Though she realized now that she probably wasn't going to college in Dallas any longer. She wanted to be near her brother, but he wasn't going to be there.

Then the chauffeur drove the limo onto a long drive and parked in front of a virtual mansion, that was akin to a castle of its own. The gardens were gorgeous, fountains out front, flowers everywhere but some of the trees were sporting beautiful fall colors too—from greens to oranges, golds, yellows, purples, and reds.

Fiona was so eager to see her brother, she threw open the limo door before the chauffeur could get it for her. Arman hurried after her. Everyone quickly exited the car and Levka said, "We have some friends who are here."

About thirty men and women came out of the mansion. Fiona felt a little panicked that they were going to be in a fight, but Levka assured her, "They're friends, making sure we're all right and we have more of a security force if Tobias or his friends show up here."

Fiona sighed with relief, but she still needed to see her brother. "Where's Justin?"

One of the vampires smiled at her. "Swimming in the pool. He's in heaven."

Fiona was so glad for it.

Caitlin said, "But we're all going to have to get some sleep to deal with jetlag."

Oh, yeah, the adrenaline had been flooding Fiona's bloodstream and she hadn't felt tired, but now that she was meeting up with her brother, she felt relieved, and exhausted.

Arman led her through the house, Levka and their little group following them until they reached the pool. She knew they wanted to meet him just as much as she wanted to see him.

As soon as she saw her brother, she called out to him, "Justin!" She was crying and ran to the edge of the pool, slipping a little, but Arman caught her arm before she fell in. That would have been so lame.

Justin smiled broadly at her and swam to the edge of the pool and pulled himself out of the water, then gave her a big wet hug. "Hey, sis."

"Omigod," Justin. She hugged him, weeping happy tears. He was alive. And she loved him. She was so glad that when the vampires had changed his memories, they hadn't wiped the memories of her from his mind.

But now she had some hard choices to make. He was a human. She was a huntress. Her parents were vampires. What was she to do? Tell him? Keep it all a secret?

Where was Justin going to go once they had eliminated the threat? Back to Dallas? She couldn't think of him going back there. Not when he had no other family than her and she wouldn't be with him to protect him in the event anyone targeted him. She would have to think about it once she had some sleep and just chilled for a few days.

"How come you are here?" Justin asked. "Did you win a trip here also? No, that would be too weird."

"I know, right? I've got to sleep, and I'll see you in a few hours?" She was soaking wet after he hugged her. But she didn't care. She was just so glad to see her brother was there and safe.

Justin smiled. "Sure." He glanced at Arman. "Who's he?" Now he was acting like a protective big brother?

"Arman. Everyone will—" She was going to say make introductions later.

Arman shook his hand. "I'm Fiona's boyfriend."

Fiona couldn't believe he would say that. Well, she guessed he was, after coming to her rescue and after all the visions she had shared with him. Though he was a vampire, and she was a huntress. Wasn't that kind of like mixing oil with water?

The other vampires were talking to Levka, and they seemed to be taking their direction from him. It was fascinating to see the dynamics between vampires. She wondered if it had to do with Levka and the other guys who were so close to him all being princes. But that was in Wales. Since this was Scotland, she wouldn't think they would owe any kind of allegiance to him.

Caitlin said to Fiona, "He's often in charge, though we all fought to help the Scots overthrow their League rulers. So they gave us this estate and they are here to watch out for you. We're glad we have some additional support if we need it."

"Do you think Regina and Tobias would send people for me?" Fiona asked.

"If what you can do is as important as they seem to think it is, yes."

"What if someone else wants to control that power? Someone here already? I don't mean at the estate, but in Scotland, if the vampires here learn of it?" Fiona wouldn't be surprised if there were rogue vampires here who would crave additional power.

"That too. So where would you like to sleep? I'm staying with Levka, of course. Jasmine is with Stasio. Arman and Ruric have their own rooms. We have plenty more for you to choose from. They're all beautiful, but..."

"You want to make sure I'm being watched," Fiona said.

"Protected."

"Tomorrow, first thing I want to start sword fighting training."

"I don't blame you. I'm going to do it with you," Caitlin said, all smiles.

"Oh, that would be great." Fiona was really glad she wasn't the only one who needed training. Doing it with Caitlin would make it a lot more fun.

"So, uhm, anyway, if you don't want to stay with one of the guys, I can stay with you, or Jasmine can, though I probably shouldn't speak for her. I'm sure she would be fine with it."

"Can I look at the unoccupied rooms?"

"Sure." Caitlin showed her one of the rooms. "This one is right next door to Arman's room. Justin's is across the hall from your room."

"I'll take it. The guys can protect me if I scream."

Caitlin shook her head. "Vampires can appear places, you know."

"Aren't there any safeguards?"

"Well, Levka and the others will make sure everyone on the staff—they're human—and the vampires here know what Regina and Tobias look like, if they should show up."

"But humans can be convinced to let them in."

"True. But some vampires will remain on guard until they're not needed any longer," Caitlin assured her.

"Okay, well, I'm going to get some sleep."

"All right. Me too. Jetlag isn't any fun." Then Caitlin gave her a hug. "I'm glad we saved you in time."

"Thanks. I am too." Fiona went into the bedroom and shut the door. She wondered if she would dream of Arman or maybe even her father. But for now, she just wanted to sleep.

As soon as she climbed into bed, she closed her eyes, but then there was a rapping at her door. "Yes?"

The door opened a crack. Arman peeked in. "Caitlin said you took the room next to mine."

"Yes. I'll just scream if anyone comes for me."

"If someone can reach you, you won't have time to call out."

"So, what? Do you think you should join me on this big king size bed…to protect me?"

"Yeah, that's exactly what I am thinking."

She laughed and pulled aside the covers. "For this afternoon. But tonight? We'll play it by ear."

"Alright." Arman looked relieved, took off his shoes, and climbed onto the bed.

"Okay, no more talking. I have to sleep."

Arman said, "Yeah, me too."

Both of them closed their eyes, but before she fell sleep, she felt Arman move closer to her and then pull her into his embrace.

"Is this a necessary part of protecting me?" she asked.

He was so cute.

"Yeah." He kissed her ear. "If anyone grabs you, I'll know it right away."

She took a deep breath, let it out, and enjoyed being here with Arman, and with the others whom she now called friends. She couldn't believe how much her life had changed in an instant. She hoped that everyone here was being truthful about everything, but she realized she had nowhere else to go and no one else she could trust. Not when humans wouldn't believe that vampires and hunters and, well, even witches existed.

"Dream of me chasing you this time," Arman sleepily said against her hair.

"I'm going to sleep and not get into anyone's dreams at all." At least she hoped not. She really needed to be well-rested if she was going to practice sword fighting tomorrow. Or maybe even after she woke from her nap. But this was so nice being with Arman. After all the craziness in her life, she finally felt safe and cared for.

ARMAN WAS glad Fiona had allowed him to stay with her because he had planned on sleeping in the chair nearby, anything, to make sure she stayed safe. He just wanted to make sure no one came for her without them being aware of it, not since they had managed to save her from Regina and Tobias. He wanted to make sure she stayed safe.

Levka spoke to him then. *"Are you staying with Fiona? Caitlin said Fiona wouldn't willingly stay with anyone, but one of us needs to always be with her."*

"I'm with her."

"Good. Talk to you when we wake."

This was so nice, like Arman's dreams, but even better. He still felt she should be one of them, but he understood her reluctance to be turned. It was more than a life-changing event. If they could get through the night of the blood moon without anyone taking control of her, she would be safer, and she probably wouldn't need to be turned at that point. But could she make it past that event without any further trouble?

Then he drifted off to sleep. *Fog surrounded Arman on a cold night as the blood moon hung high in the sky, mists of clouds drifting over it and past it. Arman couldn't figure out why he was standing outside on the estate's property surrounded by forest and gardens. He had a sinking feeling that Fiona was out there. Why else would he have left her alone? But how had he let her out of his sight? He was sweating despite the chilliness in the air.*

Levka suddenly ran across the gardens to join him. "Where is she? None of us can find her! Where is she? It's time. If we don't find her, we're—"

Swords suddenly clanked off in the distance—someone was fighting with someone else near the edge of the woods. If Fiona was fighting someone on her own after so few sword-fighting lessons, she would be at an extreme disadvantage. Levka vanished and Arman did the same thing. But they didn't go immediately to the woods. Both had to retrieve their swords.

He wanted to save Fiona. He had to rescue her. But then...

Something clicked. His eyes shot open. Fiona was gone. The click he'd heard was the sound of the door closing on her departure from the bedroom, he thought. He hurried out of bed and put on his shoes. And then he yanked the door open and rushed out the door. He caught up to her heading downstairs and she smiled at him.

"You were sound asleep, and I didn't want to wake you."

"I had a bad dream. Or vision."

Her smile slipped. "What happened?"

"It was the night of the blood moon, and you were gone. Levka joined me and we heard sword fighting and both of us went to grab our swords, but then you woke me."

She frowned at him. "Oh, great. I wish I hadn't woken you." She paused at the base of the stairs. "Do you think it was me fighting with someone?"

"That's what we worried about. Did you have any dreams or visions?"

"No. Not at all. I was so tired, I think I just slept."

"Okay, well, damn. I wish I had seen what happened next." Then Arman heard Levka downstairs, and they smelled chicken. "Time to eat."

"I'm sorry. I wish there was a way you could tell me you were in the middle of a dream or a vision and I could join you or at the very least, not disturb you while you're in the middle of it."

"Maybe it will come to me again tonight when we go to sleep and I'll see more of the dream or vision." As soon as they walked into the dining room, Arman asked Levka, "Did you have a dream?"

"Not that I recall. Oh, yeah, Caitlin and I were making gingerbread cookies. I have no idea why. I don't like gingerbread and I've never made cookies in my life."

Arman laughed. He couldn't imagine Levka baking cookies.

But Caitlin said, "Why? Did you have a dream about Levka?" She wasn't smiling, appearing more worried than anything.

"Yeah. We were looking for Fiona. I'm sure we were all trying to find her. Then we heard sword fighting."

"And then?" Caitlin asked.

"Sorry. It's my fault. I accidentally woke him, and he didn't see any more. I mean, it could be just a dream, not a premonition of things to come." Fiona took a seat at the table next to Arman.

Ruric entered the dining room. "In the dream, when did it occur and where?"

"Here at the estate, outside, during the night of the blood moon. It's foggy out and partly cloudy," Arman said.

Jasmine and Stasio joined them, and Jasmine said, "Now what?"

Arman explained what he had dreamed or seen, and Jasmine shook her head. "Okay, after lunch, we work on sword fighting. I thought it could wait until tomorrow, but time is of the essence. If Fiona has to fight a vampire, she needs as much training as she can get."

"Oh, I agree," Fiona said. "I want to get started right away."

"Me too," Caitlin said. "I need lots more practice."

Michail and Shelly joined them too, and soon Justin did also.

Justin smiled. "The food is so great here. It's like fine dining all the time. I keep thinking I'll wake up from the dream."

"I'm just so glad to see you," Fiona said. "How much do you know about what happened to our mom and dad?"

Arman wondered too about what he had been told.

"Michail told me that they had died in a car accident. I figured it would be coming because of the way dad drank. I wasn't surprised to learn it at all. I was sorry to hear it though. Mom deserved a better life. The first thing I wanted to know though was where you were and why no one had told me that they had died."

"I sent letters to you. But...I guess you didn't get any of them," Fiona said. "I just figured you were too busy to write back or call me. I could never get ahold of you, and I couldn't leave any messages on your voicemail."

"I was busy, but I would have called you back. I never received any letters. Michail said you were staying at a great aunt's house, but I had no idea who she was. But he said you were coming here, so I figured I would see you then and get all the details."

"She wasn't our relation. She lied about it." But Fiona didn't tell her brother that they weren't truly related.

"What the hell. Why?"

Now that would be hard to explain. Arman wondered what Fiona was going to say about that.

"I thought it might have to do with an inheritance or something, but I have no idea." Fiona began eating some of her chicken.

"We're going to go out and do some sword fighting after lunch," Jasmine said to Justin. "You should come too and practice."

"Like fencing?" Justin said.

"Like medieval longsword fighting," Arman said.

Justin smiled. "Oh, that sounds like fun."

"You'll get a workout for sure." Arman wanted him to know it wasn't a game. He wished they could warn Justin about the danger Fiona was faced with. They'd had to tell Fiona because her life was up for grabs.

After they had chicken, green beans, and fried potatoes, they all went to the armory to grab their swords. Arman gave Fiona a training sword. Caitlin had one also. They gave one to Justin, but he was looking over the real swords and Arman could just guess he wanted one of those. But he had to learn the right way to hold one and he might not have the time to get good enough to fight with a real sword.

Michail and Shelly said they would watch. Arman was kind of surprised to hear it. Most vampires, or hunters for that matter, would take every opportunity to hone their skills in the event they had to use them.

Fiona looked eager to fight. So did Caitlin and Justin. Arman smiled. That's what they needed. Fire in their hearts. The determination to put in a good fight. Even Justin might need to use a sword if it came to that. But Arman really hoped he wouldn't.

"You didn't tell Michail and Shelly about your dream," Fiona said telepathically to Arman while they were watching Levka and Ruric showing the key movements, how to parry, thrust, stand, and hold the sword.

"No. I think it's best if we keep it among ourselves. They came down late for lunch and so did Justin. He shouldn't know for certain, but I think it's just safer if we don't tell Michail and Shelly about our visions or dreams or whatever they are."

"You don't trust them. But they saved my brother."

"Yeah, but I would rather be safe than sorry. When your parents arrive and confirm they are friends of theirs like they say, I'll be convinced."

"Oh, you think they might have saved my brother on Regina's orders? And then brought him here to sneak in like offering a Trojan Horse?" Fiona sounded shocked.

"Anything is possible when it comes to powerful vampires. Regina could have learned that we fought with the Scots to overthrow the League here."

"Okay. Do the others know to keep quiet about it?"

Arman took hold of Fiona's hand and squeezed it with reassurance. "Yeah. We all have lived for so long, it's instinctual."

"Oh, sure, that makes sense."

He hoped he wasn't distracting her from watching the sword fighting lesson, but she'd asked an important question of him, and he had needed to ensure she knew not to mention any dreams or visions she might have in front of the sister and brother. He should have thought of it before, but he'd been so tired when they first got in, he had forgotten about it.

"So what do you think of the sword fighting?" he asked her.

"I'm eager to try it."

He smiled. "It looks like your brother is really ready to try it." He watched him parroting Levka and Ruric's moves with his practice sword and was really getting into it.

Then it was time for the newbies to begin practicing and Arman paired up with Fiona. Ruric was showing Justin the moves. Levka was working with Caitlin again. She really was getting better at it. She knew the stances and she knew the sword movements. But what he was really surprised at was that Fiona was really capable of handling a sword.

15

Stasio, Michail, and Shelly were watching the rest of them practice at sword fighting, though Fiona was trying to concentrate on the mission—training and being the best she could be. Just like when she was training in martial arts and doing sword demonstrations. She was amused at seeing Arman's look of awe and surprise when she could wield a sword so well. This came naturally to her, and she was really enjoying the workout. She wasn't tired at all like she thought she would be. She hadn't done martial arts in the time since she had moved to Portland.

But using a sword to end a vampire, that was a whole other story. She wasn't sure she could do that. Then again, if a vampire was trying to kill her, she wasn't going to just allow it. She still couldn't believe she had disturbed Arman from the vision he was having. Or a dream. She wished they could know which it was. They wouldn't know though until they had some confirmation. Like she was missing, everyone was searching for her on the night of the blood moon, and she was involved in a sword fight. Or maybe she wasn't. Maybe it was one of the other people in their little party who was off fighting.

She hoped that Arman would see more in another dream that would help them pinpoint what was going on. Or that maybe she would. She had no intention of leaving the mansion on her own.

Her brother was taking a break and watching her now. So was Ruric. Then Caitlin and Levka took a break and observed Arman and Fiona practicing. When they finally finished, everyone clapped. Fiona smiled. She enjoyed that they thought she was halfway competent to wield a sword.

They went inside to get some refreshments.

"You did great," Caitlin said. "I've been practicing for over a year to get to where I am and wow, I am so impressed at how well you did for your first time at it."

Justin agreed. "I was the real newbie at this. I should have taken martial arts like you did, Fiona."

"Yeah, but you've got muscles," Jasmine said. "So once you get the moves down and they come naturally, you can really put those muscles to work on strong swings."

Which reminded Fiona why they were here, and she kept thinking Justin shouldn't be. That he would be safer if he wasn't near her.

They all headed inside to get some refreshments.

"Do you think my brother should be somewhere else? Somewhere that might be safer?" she asked Arman.

"He needs to be here if he's to be safe. If Regina were to get to him, she could force you to return to come to his rescue. This is where he needs to be," Arman reassured her.

"Okay, I just wanted to be sure."

Some of the kitchen staff brought them tea and shortbread cookies, then left them alone. The friends began drinking the assortments of tea from Scotch to heather and having cookies in the living room when Fiona looked at the new phone they had gotten her and realized Justin had to have his phone too. What if

Regina and Tobias could find him through that? *"What about Justin's phone? Could they find him that way?"*

Justin was just then looking at his phone.

Arman asked, "Hey, is that a new phone?"

"Uh, yeah. That was part of what I won on this trip. But...you all won a trip here also? That's sounds like way too much of a coincidence," Justin said to Fiona.

"Levka is a friend, and he knew I wanted to see you, so he arranged this whole vacation for you, for me, and some of our friends," Fiona said, figuring it was time to change the story to one that made a little more sense, but she didn't know how long they could keep the charade going.

"Wow, that's amazing," Justin said. "Well, I'm glad for it. I'm having a blast. I'm just thrilled that I had the free time to come here and get to see you too."

Which wasn't really the truth. Winter break hadn't arrived yet, so he was missing out on his coursework, and she hated that for him. But she was glad that he had a new phone and couldn't be tracked. Michail and Shelly must have thought of that. Which had to make them good guys also. At least she sure hoped so. But what if they gave Justin a phone that Regina had authorized?

"Hey, who wants to go swimming?" Justin asked.

"I'm with you," Jasmine said. "I don't have any assignments right now."

"If you're going swimming, so am I," Stasio said.

The princes had given Levka a bit of a hard time over his interest in Caitlin, but that was before Stasio and Jasmine ended up being a couple.

"Do you want to go swimming?" Fiona asked Arman. She knew they had to stick together, or at least they should.

"Yeah, sure. Let's do it."

"Great." She was so glad she'd picked out a couple of bathing suits. The pool looked so inviting and she couldn't wait to swim with the others, but especially with Arman.

They all headed up to their rooms and got changed, Arman giving Fiona some space, but once she was dressed in her swimsuit, and had her coverup on, she found Arman coming to escort her. He was already dressed in blue swim trunks featuring hammerhead sharks. She laughed when she saw them. "So you're a shark."

He smiled and looked over her blue one-piece bathing suit. "We match. Minus the sharks, of course."

She laughed. When they arrived at the pool, Justin was already diving in and Levka and Caitlin were together at one end of the pool, kissing each other. Jasmine and Stasio soon jumped into the pool. Ruric jumped in and splashed everyone. They splashed him back, laughing, enjoying the moment.

Fiona slipped into the water and Arman jumped in after her. She waited for him, thinking they could swim laps, but she wanted to see what he wished to do.

Arman swam over to her and smiled. "We haven't been at the estate for very long, and though I've swum in the pool a couple of times, I never thought I would be swimming with you—"

"The girl who spilled her soda all over you."

"Absolutely. I was afraid you would think we stalked you all the way to Dallas."

"I did consider that. But you waited two whole years to do it? I mean, yeah, seeing you and your friends was way too much of a coincidence, but still, it didn't make any sense. And my dreams of you? They were never a nightmare but the most pleasant of dreams."

"Until that one night and I knew I was there with you and the blond guy warned me you were in danger, and I had to save you."

"If he is the same one, he told me to trust you. But he didn't say who you were. I asked, and then he was gone. Like something had broken the connection. But even if he had told me your name, I might not have believed him, or trusted him."

"So swooping in and carrying you away from the school had been the only way to handle it."

She smiled at Arman as they both paddled in the warm water. "Yeah, that worked. Though at the time, I had serious doubts about you and the others." She looked around to see where Michail and Shelly were, but they hadn't joined them. "Do you think they feel like they're not part of the group?"

"Who?"

"Michail and Shelly?" Fiona asked.

"Maybe. We're a tightknit group. It takes us a while to trust others. I'm sure they realize that, and we might make them a little uncomfortable," Arman said.

"That could be. The people here who make the meals and clean the rooms, are they all human?" Fiona asked.

"Yeah. They're paid well. They're not blood bonds like some of the humans are in other vampire households."

"Blood bonds?" she asked.

"Blood blonds work for vampires, but they also allow the vampires to feed off them."

"Oh." Fiona wouldn't like that one bit.

"They're not forced to do it. Which would make the vampires rogues. The blood bonds do it for the money and for the enjoyment they get out of it," Arman said.

"I can't imagine."

He just smiled, drew closer, and kissed her. She welcomed the kiss and wrapped her arms around his neck, while he kicked his legs in the pool to keep them both afloat. "Kissing you is so much better than in our dreams."

"I agree."

The butler came out to the swimming pool and said, "You have company."

"Who?" Arman asked.

"He says he's Stasio's cousin, Prince Gareth. And Jasmine's brother, Brett, is here also. They both learned you are in trouble again and came to help you out." The butler cast him a wry smile.

"Thanks." Arman was about to shout to Stasio, who was swimming under the water with Jasmine, when Gareth hurried out to the pool, yanked off all but his boxer shorts, and did a cannonball into the water.

Brett had been right behind him, but he walked to the edge of the pool, folded his arms, and smiled.

His job done here, the butler headed back into the house.

Then Brett looked at Fiona and shook his head. "Don't tell me you have convinced another woman to join your pack."

"She's a huntress," Arman said, "but she never knew it. Her parents were turned."

Brett's expression changed from amused to worried.

Arman nodded. "Yeah, she's in trouble."

"I had heard you and your friends were in trouble, which is why I'm here," Brett said.

"We're training her how to use a sword, but—"

"I'm a black belt in three forms of martial arts and have been trained to use a sword or two in demonstrations."

Brett raised his brows. "But not in a fight to the death."

"You can help train her since you're a hunter too," Arman said.

"Yeah, but she doesn't need to fight one of my kind. She needs to know how to fight one of yours," Brett said.

Fiona realized what Brett said was true.

Jasmine and Stasio came up for air and they saw Gareth swimming out to them.

Brett called out to them, "Hey, so when's the fight coming?"

"Ohmigod, Brett. You didn't tell me you were on your way here," Jasmine said, hurrying to the side of the pool and climbing out. She gave him a big hug and got him all wet, just like Justin had done to Fiona when she first saw him in the pool last night.

"So you both came here to help us out?" Fiona was amazed.

"Yeah."

"Even a hunter? I guess because he's Jasmine's brother."

Then the butler returned with two more guests. "Prince Cadfael and Prince Llewellyn have also just arrived, my prince."

Arman said, "Good to see you, Cadfael, Llewellyn."

"As soon as Gareth said you were in trouble and needed help, we were on our way." Llewellyn glanced at Fiona. "And you are the source of all the trouble?"

"Fiona...uh, Fairhaven. Glad to make your acquaintance." She guessed.

"They are hunters also. So is Fiona," Arman said, sounding like he hated mentioning it again to other hunters.

Both of the men smiled at her. She assumed they were bachelors, and that the guys might be interested in a huntress to date. But she was so hooked on a hot-blooded vampire, she really wasn't interested in dating hunters. *Go figure.*

Her brother was swimming laps and didn't hear the conversation or notice that anyone else had arrived. Talking about upcoming fights and hunters would really have him wondering what was going on.

Brett, Cadfael, and Llewellyn declined swimming and sat poolside having drinks. Later, it was time to get out of the pool for the rest of them, dry off, and change.

"Lunch, right?" Cadfael said. "Levka said your chef does a great job on meals, which was the main reason we came."

Everyone laughed.

16

Arman couldn't believe that all these bachelor hunters had shown up to help protect Fiona. He was glad for it as far as keeping her safe, but not as far as her finding someone else to be interested in. Which was not fair in the least to Fiona. She was a huntress, and she would do well to be with other hunters as much as Arman hated the idea. If she had a hunter in her life, he could continue to protect her until she had the fighting skills that she needed to protect herself.

Arman glanced at Levka, who inclined his head to him. Levka would know just what Arman was thinking, but he also acknowledged he understood. Arman sighed.

Fiona saw the exchange and took hold of Arman's hand and squeezed it. She said to him, "Don't worry. I'm not running off with one of the hunters. I don't dream about *them*."

He smiled at her, but still, he couldn't help feeling that it wouldn't work out between them. He would live well beyond her short life. He needed a vampire mate. But he didn't want to turn her unless she practically begged him to.

Even so, he made sure that he kept Fiona as far from the hunters as he could at the table, and his friends had helped to make that happen too. He saw the smiles on Gareth and his brothers' faces, indicating that they were totally amused to see the vampires protecting Fiona from them.

Arman wished Justin knew what was going on. He was the only human at the table and so clueless. It was going to be hard to keep the secret of what they all were from him, Arman believed.

Michail and Shelly showed up and sat down to eat at the table with everyone, while introductions were made all around. They told Gareth and his brothers how they had brought Justin here so he could see his sister and that he had won some money and the trip here.

Arman was sure Levka had filled the brothers in on all that was going on. But he was just as sure Levka hadn't told Michail and Shelly that he had invited the hunters to the party, so to speak.

Once they had eaten fish and chips, they all headed out to do more weapons training.

"I'm glad we're practicing sword fighting again," Caitlin said. "I need to keep working at it just in case I need it for a fight in the future."

"That goes for me too now," Fiona said. "I guess. I mean, I took martial arts because I liked it and I thought I might be able to use it to defend myself, but not quite like this."

"You'll do great," Arman said to Fiona, wanting to encourage her every step of the way.

Llewellyn said to Fiona, "As hunters, we can show you how we fight, but we think it's just as beneficial or even more so to train to fight against vampires, since that's who will most likely target you as a hunter. If you have to protect yourself against a hunter, you'll still learn enough by fighting the vampires. Though we'll be happy to put you through your paces."

"We understand you have never been around hunters your entire life," Cadfael said.

"Correct. I didn't even know hunters or vampires existed," Fiona said.

Justin was standing there listening to the whole conversation when Arman realized the mistake that was made. They'd been so careful not to discuss being vampires, or hunters, around him, but it was practically impossible. Earlier at the pool, Justin had been so far away and swimming laps so vigorously, he hadn't heard their conversations about hunters. Arman had known this would happen!

"Vampires?" Justin said. "Hunters? You mean like Van Helsing?"

"No. Van Helsing was human," Cadfael said. "And he's only fictional. Some humans hunt vampires, sure. But mostly hunters hunt rogue vampires. Some hunters also take down rogue hunters." He explained how hunters and vampires came to be during the time of the Black Death.

It was too late to keep Justin in the dark any further.

"No way." Justin sounded like he thought they were just playing a game.

"I was born to vampire parents," Jasmine said. "The princes were turned."

"During the Black Death?" Justin smiled, like he knew they were joking.

"Yeah," Arman said. "We've been around for a while." He suspected if Justin believed them and they weren't just playing a joke on him or role playing or something, that he wouldn't like that his sister was interested in Arman, just because of the age difference. Though Arman's being a vampire too, that could be a real point of contention.

"How come I've never seen any of your fangs?" Justin asked.

"You don't want to see them," Fiona said.

Arman didn't know how she was feeling about her brother knowing. She'd come around pretty quickly to learning what they were, but she was a hunter with a special power. Her brother was only human with all the frailties of his kind.

Fiona released her breath. "Alright, everyone who has them, show my brother your fangs. He needs to know what we're potentially up against during the blood moon."

All the vampires showed their extended canines, but Caitlin, though Arman knew it was because she just couldn't show them off whenever she wanted to unless she was angry. The display by all the vampires there was really impressive, Arman thought.

Justin's jaw dropped, but then he smiled. And like Fiona, Justin said, "You guys are really into this, aren't you? Weird, but cool. Dental implants? They look real."

The vampires, except for Caitlin, all hid their fangs.

Justin appeared to be a little puzzled at that. Implants couldn't disappear.

Then Arman nodded to the rest of his friends, and the vampires all just...vanished.

"Now do you believe them?" Fiona asked. "Not that it didn't take some convincing for me also."

"It's...it's some kind of trick," Justin said.

Arman didn't blame Justin for not believing in it. Arman and his friends reappeared, but farther away. Then they flew back to where Justin and the hunters were standing. Even Caitlin had gone with the vampires that time. She had more trouble with her canines, but with vanishing and flying, she was getting to be a pro.

Arman glanced over at Justin. He was sitting down on the ground, looking as though he'd fallen where he'd been standing, his mouth agape.

"Are you okay?" Fiona asked, rushing over to help him up,

but he was too wobbly, and he couldn't stand. She sat down beside him.

"If you're a hunter and I'm a human, that means we're not related?" Justin asked, tears in his eyes. He appeared really shaken by all this.

"We're brother and sister, but maybe not by blood," Fiona said.

Arman knew she had to tell him all of it at this point. When and if they had a fight with vampires while they were protecting her, they had to make sure that Justin knew what was going on and stayed safe if they were to keep him here.

"Your parents aren't the same as mine?" Justin asked.

"No. I was given to your parents to raise, and I never knew my own."

"What about Uncle Nat and Aunt Bea?"

"I believe they might have been my parents, and they were paying for a lot of our things over the years, treating us like we were sister and brother and their niece and nephew."

"Where are they now? If you knew about all this, did you know about that too?" Justin sounded upset with her.

"I didn't know about any of this. Not until Arman and his friends came into my life to rescue me. My parents are coming here." Then Fiona explained about the dream business.

"Do you believe any of this?" Justin asked.

"I do. I have to. Not only are the others here to protect me, they're here to protect you too."

"Is that why Michail and Shelly came to get me? I thought I had won a trip here. And to see you? None of that's true? Are you sure?"

"Yeah, except about seeing me. They wanted you to be protected too."

Justin glanced at all the vampires and hunters there.

"We're here for you," Cadfael said. "For you and your sister."

Arman was glad he had called Fiona Justin's sister. Justin had already lost his own parents and even his sister in the deal, not to mention the world he knew had just been turned inside out.

"Some of the vampires are willing to turn you so that you have more abilities and the longevity they have," Fiona said, glad they had told her brother the truth, but she thought he was still having a hard time believing in all of it.

"And the blood drinking need?" Justin asked.

Fiona hugged him. "Yeah, that's the biggest drawback."

"What about you? Wouldn't it help for you to also be a vampire?" Justin asked.

"They've suggested that also."

"I'll do it if you do it," Justin said.

Fiona smiled. "I'm just getting used to being a hunter and having some kind of idea about the dreams."

"What can you do with them?" Justin asked.

"I don't know yet." She still was not comfortable with Shelly and Michail listening in. She felt the others were truly behind her all the way. She just wasn't sure about the two new vampires. She didn't think that Arman or his friends were intent on anything but protecting her. She thought when her parents arrived, they could vouch for Shelly and Michail and she would feel better about it.

"Let's uhm, practice fighting then," Justin said, "if we're going to have a fight for our lives during the blood moon. Here I thought we were just going to celebrate your birthday."

"Oh, speaking of that, Arman, Caitlin, and I are making plans. If you want to come with us tomorrow before we are doing our sword practice," Jasmine said to Justin, "you can let us know what Fiona likes."

Fiona knew they could have a real fight on their hands with other vampires on her birthday. She never thought of anyone throwing a birthday party for her!

"Yeah, sure, I would love to do that," Justin said, finally standing and helping Fiona up. Then he hugged her. "You're right. We're still brother and sister, though we might have another difference between us soon."

"Oh?" Being human and hunter was enough of a difference, Fiona thought.

"Vampire and hunter. I can't be turned into a hunter, can I?" Justin asked.

Fiona hadn't thought of that.

"No. Only vampires can turn humans…or hunters. But hunters have to be born that way," Levka said.

Then they all paired up to fight each other—Cadfael, Llewellyn, and Gareth taking turns with Arman to give Fiona a workout, showing her the difference between hunters and vampires, and even between each of the hunters who had their own style of fighting.

"Wow," Fiona said. "I would never have realized how different you all fight. It really gives me the disadvantage. I think Cadfael will be the same as Llewellyn, and then I fight him, and he throws me off completely. The same with Gareth. And of course the vampires are the same way with their unique maneuvers."

"For being so new at this, you adapt really well," Arman said. "I don't believe I've ever had to train anyone in sword fighting who can learn and anticipate new moves so quickly."

"I agree," Gareth said. "You would make a great vampire assassin."

"There's good money in it too," Jasmine said. "Next time we practice, you and I will have a go at it."

Fiona knew Jasmine would be just as hard on her as the guys

had been. They couldn't go easy on her, not with the dangers she faced.

"Is everyone ready for dinner?" Levka finally asked.

Everyone unanimously wanted to have dinner.

They'd worked out for a couple of hours and were ready for the break, and everyone retired to the house.

"We're making dinner," Levka said. "Guys on the grills. We'll do it all."

"Wow, really?" Fiona asked.

"Yeah. We'll need to do our own laundry, keep our own rooms cleaned, look after ourselves," Levka said.

Arman asked, "You let the human staff go?"

"Aye. They're too easily influenced. They've been given two weeks' vacation in the Cayman Islands. They'll have a good time, and they won't be hurt or eliminated if the wrong vampires show up here and they were to let them in," Levka said.

"Good idea," Arman said.

"We're used to taking care of ourselves," Ruric said, "though in the future, robots could do all of it. And they couldn't be controlled by rogue vampires."

"But they could be controlled by a rogue vampire hacker," Stasio said.

Everyone laughed.

"Have you had any further word from my parents?" Fiona asked Michail and his sister.

Why wouldn't her parents contact her, not the other vampires?

"Not yet," Shelly said. "They've been trying to stay off the grid in case Tobias wants to still take your dad as a hostage and control him. I'm sure they'll be here in no time at all, especially before the day of the blood moon."

Then the guys all went out back where several grills were

situated on a large stone patio and they began to grill hamburgers and corn on the cob.

Jasmine said to Fiona, "I thought Justin took the business of us being vampires well, didn't you?"

"After he got over the initial shock, yes. It sounds like he wants to be turned, but he might have just been joking about it," Fiona said. "I don't want him turned just because someone thought he truly meant it when he didn't."

"Right," Caitlin said. "For me, it was a life or death matter, so an easy choice to make. But it was also forbidden by the League of Vampires, so Levka was in trouble for that."

"Oh, I didn't know that," Fiona said.

"Not here in Scotland because we overthrew the old rulers," Jasmine said. "We have a new League of Vampire's Bill of Rights, and turning someone in the case where it's mutually agreeable is perfectly acceptable."

"Oh," Fiona said. Here she'd thought that Arman's offer of turning her was legal and he wouldn't be in any conflict for it. But from the sounds of it, only Scotland allowed for it. So if they stayed in Scotland, they were fine, but if they left the country, that would be another story. She didn't want Arman or any of the others to get into any issues over her. Then again, wasn't that another reason they had been in trouble? For helping hunters or humans out when they should be left to fend for themselves?

17

After dinner, Justin was shown to his room next to Ruric's and everyone retired to bed.

Arman was staying with Fiona, and she was glad Justin hadn't made an issue of it, though she suspected he was glad Arman was there to protect her.

She had finally drifted off to sleep with Arman and thought she might be with him in her dreams.

But then she found herself in a darkened area with dim streetlights and warehouse buildings when she saw Levka and the other princes telling some thugs to release a couple of teen girls they were hassling. Before she could fathom what was going on, one of the brutish guys aimed to shoot at the girl and Levka vanished and appeared between the gunman and the girl, taking three bullets to protect her.

Ohmigod, this was too awful. Levka was in bad shape, but his friends quickly took care of the thugs and ferreted the girls to safety. Levka began dreaming of the nightmare again, as if he was in a continuous loop and he couldn't stop reliving the terror. Fiona jumped in, making herself appear like a dragon, breathing fire and sending the thugs screaming off into night.

Levka just stared at her. The girls fainted. She didn't see any of his friends as if it was just Levka and her. Then he dreamed he was on a cruise ship meeting Caitlin, and worried about her because some teen guy was threatening her. But Levka had been wounded—and Fiona realized it was from being shot. Dang it. She had to change the scenario and she tossed the bully off the ship and smiled.

Then Arman and the others soon joined them and before Fiona was ready for it, Levka was kissing Caitlin and Fiona smiled. She figured his nightmares, hopefully, were over for the night.

She woke herself up and wrote the dream down so she could ask Arman about it tomorrow.

But then she closed her eyes and tried to search for anyone else's dreams she might find. Like Shelly and Michail's. Dreams could be so crazy and mixed up. She wasn't sure if they were really the truth or just something nonsensical. Yet she sensed the dreams her friends had were things that had actually happened to them and were reoccurring nightmares. What if she could learn something important about Shelly or her brother? Now that would be truly cool.

The next thing Fiona knew was she was chasing after Arman and laughing hysterically. She couldn't catch him until he suddenly stopped and turned, and she collided with him. He swept her up in his arms and kissed her. Now this was more like it!

THE NEXT MORNING, Fiona woke and heard Arman in the bathroom showering. She dressed and called out, "I'll see you downstairs."

The shower shut off and Arman came out of the bathroom wearing a towel around his waist, his skin glistening with water, his smile on the devilish side.

She chuckled. "Good morning. I'll save us a seat at the dining room table."

"Morning." He smiled and pulled her into a hug and kissed her. And got her all wet!

"You're not worried that I'll be out of your sight for a few minutes, are you?"

"No. From the nightmare or the premonition that I had where you had disappeared, it was at night. So as long as you don't slip away from me at night, I think we're good. And as long as you're with one of the others and not on your own."

She kissed him back. "You only hugged me so I could help dry you off."

He laughed. "You know me too well already. I'll dress and be down in a minute."

"Was Levka shot helping a couple of teen girls?"

Arman stared at Fiona for a moment. "Did you dream of it?"

"Yeah, he was having a nightmare about it."

"Oh, yeah, and then we had to flee on a cruise ship."

"Right, and then he had to save Caitlin."

"Were you able to help Levka with his nightmare?"

"Of course. I turned into a fire-breathing dragon."

Arman laughed. "Now that I would like to see. I'll be downstairs in a jif."

Which she took to mean he would just appear there, no walking the distance. She thought that was really cool when they had to move quickly. He would have beat her there, if it hadn't been that he had to dress first. No speed in dressing.

Even so, by the time she reached the dining room, seconds later, there was Arman, her favorite vampire in the world. He clasped her hand and smiled down at her. His hair was still wet. She wanted to laugh at him for hurrying to join her so quickly.

Of course *everyone* noticed. She wondered if her parents would even accept that she was dating him. Would they approve? Then again, they hadn't raised her, they didn't know her, it was her life to live. And Arman had come to her rescue.

They took their seats at the table and waffles, porridge, haddock, and sausages were on the menu. Everyone was kind of quiet and Fiona suspected it was because tomorrow was her birthday, and the blood moon would appear in all its blood red glory.

Fiona hoped her parents would arrive on time to help them in their time of need. She desperately wanted to see them and hoped that she could get to know them. But what if they weren't anything like she hoped for? What if they didn't feel the same need to be with her that she felt with them? Would they even treat her brother like one of their own, though he wasn't? She wasn't giving up on her brother and if they didn't accept him too, she didn't know how she would deal with that.

She wondered how they would feel about Justin if he was turned into one of their kind now. Maybe they would feel a deeper connection to him, actually. Maybe *she* would be the one who wasn't like them. Or maybe they would even be saddened to think of what they had lost by no longer being hunters themselves.

Everyone began to eat. They were all pretty quiet. Then Justin spoke up. "Okay, so are we going to talk about the elephant in the room or not?"

"You better not be talking about me," Fiona said.

"I am. About your birthday, which should be the best time ever, but because of the blood moon..." Justin shook his head.

Fiona figured she wasn't going to sleep tonight, worried about tomorrow. But she also knew she needed to be well-rested if she was going to have to fight.

"We're all here for Fiona," Gareth said. "We'll do everything we can to keep her safe. And to keep you safe too."

She appreciated that Stasio's cousins were there for her and her brother also.

Justin lifted his chin. "If I were a vampire, I could help her, protect her better, protect myself better so others won't have to waste their energy trying to protect a human."

Arman sighed deeply. "It's a big change to make."

"I know. But I mean, if I don't become one, then what? I'll be like the staff here? Humans who do your bidding?" Justin sounded annoyed.

"We pay them well," Levka said. "Better than they could get at other households for the work they do. They get lots of time off, more than other places would give them. They do well."

"I just mean they know what you are. I can't unknow this stuff. I'm like them now is all I'm saying. But I don't want to be them. I want to feel in control of my life, like I thought I had been before I knew all about vampires and hunters and that I was only...only a lame human. No disrespect to humans, really. But I want to have more of an impact with my life."

"Sometimes it's a pain to be a vampire," Caitlin said. "When I feel undernourished and sluggish, weak, before I have to feed again. That I have to hide that I'm drinking blood. That I still can't do everything that a vampire can do. It's not like it's an automatic cure all for life, though to be sure there are a lot of benefits."

Fiona was glad Caitlin spoke up, being the most newly turned vampire. She would know what it felt like as compared to the others who had been turned during the Black Death or born to vampires.

Arman suddenly vanished from his seat and Fiona wondered what was up. Then Levka left in the same way, and she hoped there wasn't trouble. *"Arman, is everything okay?"* She might not be able to travel like they could, but at least she could still telepathically communicate with the others.

"Yeah, Levka and I are coming. We have...some new guests."

Could Fiona even chance hoping they were her parents? *"Mom and Dad?"*

"You'll see."

"Arman." Fiona had had enough secrets in her life, she didn't need any more, but because he didn't say no, she assumed her parents had arrived. Her hands were clammy and she felt shivers trail down her spine all at once.

A pretty blond of about thirty with riveting green eyes walked into the dining room, who totally resembled Fiona in height, her large eyes, and her heart-shaped face. She was wearing blue jeans and a T-shirt that featured a wolf with vampire fangs. Fiona raised her brows.

"I was turned against my will," the woman said to Justin.

Fiona assumed she had overheard the conversations about Justin wanting to be a vampire. Fiona heard the hurt in the woman's voice, and she couldn't imagine the terror she must have felt, or even the guilt she might have felt for turning her own beloved husband after that. To protect him, sure, but still, they'd been hunters.

"Are...are you my mother?" Fiona's eyes filled with tears.

The woman turned and smiled sweetly at Fiona, her own eyes filled with tears.

Fiona immediately got up from her chair, hesitant to give her a hug in the event she was wrong or that if the woman was her mother, she wasn't a huggable type or wasn't ready to share any intimacy with Fiona.

"I am, Beatrice Fairhaven, and I love you, Fiona," the woman said, pulling her into a hug. "It was the hardest thing for me to do—to give you up to a human family to save you. We knew Tobias would take you hostage and keep you until you turned eighteen and then turn you. All Nat and I could do was pay for things for you and Justin. We thought you were safe. That your human parents would keep you safe."

"Where is my father?"

A blond-haired man walked into the dining room and smiled at Fiona. She recognized him from her dreams/visions. "You are..."

"Nathaniel Fairhaven, your father. We have longed to see you all your life, but now it's time for us to stand united with the others here to fight the ones who—"

"Turned my mother?" Fiona asked, giving her father a hug.

He warmly embraced her back. "Yes." Then he glanced at Arman.

Everyone had risen from their seats and welcomed the couple, shaking Nat's hand, embracing Bea.

"You've come just in time for Fiona's birthday," Arman said.

"And to protect her during the blood moon," Bea said, taking hold of Fiona's hand and squeezing it. "Have you thought of being turned, Fiona?"

"Everyone's talked to me about it," Fiona said.

"I want to be turned," Justin said.

"It will change you forever, and you might not need to be, though to us, you are our adopted son, Justin," Bea said. "We love you just as much as we love Fiona. You have been good for her all these years."

Fiona was so glad her mother had said that about Justin.

"I'm ready. Really. If I can help my baby sister in this fight with the evil vampires, I'm ready for it," Justin said, sounding as serious as could be.

"Do you realize if one of us bites you, that you are controlled by that person? Not that we would make you do what we want, but it's just there is a condition to it," Bea said.

"Like Tobias bit you," Fiona said.

"Yes. So I can't kill him. And if he were here, he could try to have me do his bidding," Bea said.

"I trust you to bite me," Justin said to Bea. "I just want to have a fighting chance. I won't otherwise. I would be easy pickings."

"It's for life, however long that is," Nat said.

"Then one of you, any of you, do it."

"I'll do it," Shelly said.

Fiona shook her head. "Turn me, Arman, and I'll turn my brother."

Justin laughed. "And then *you* would control me."

Fiona smiled. "You don't want to wait until a woman who could be your mate comes for you?"

"There's no time for that. I trust you or Bea to do it. Or Nat. Really, any of your friends."

"Like I said, I'll offer," Shelly said, smiling.

Fiona wanted to ask him if he was sure of doing this, one more time, but she knew he wanted to be close to the others and felt he would be if he made the change. And she knew he wanted to help her like he couldn't as a human. She gave him a quick hug before he was no longer just her human brother. "Love you."

"I love you too. I'm going to help you the best way that I can." Then Justin gave her a hug back and said to Bea, "Will it change me so much that I can't go shopping with the others for Fiona's birthday party? We were going to go after breakfast."

"No, but you can wait to do it after you return," Bea said.

Fiona hoped Justin wasn't making a mistake. Not that she thought being a vampire was all bad, but he might decide he really didn't like being one after all and there was no changing his mind after her mother turned him.

"Yeah, I'll wait until after I return," Justin said, "just in case."

"Okay."

Then Caitlin, Jasmine, and Justin took their dishes into the kitchen. Arman gave Fiona a hug and kiss. "Be back in a little while to practice sword fighting. Just stay with the others. Don't go anywhere by yourself."

"I'll be with the others at all times. I want to get to know my parents too."

"I would go with you to shop," her mother said, "but if Tobias got a hold of me..."

"No, we understand," Fiona said. She wanted to eliminate Tobias for that reason alone. Her mother didn't feel she was safe around her and Fiona wanted to do things with her to make up for lost time.

"Of course." Arman hugged her again. "Be back soon."

Fiona knew he was worried about leaving her for any length of time, but she also knew he wanted to have some input into her birthday celebration and she loved him for it. Then Arman and the others left the house.

ARMAN DIDN'T WANT to leave Fiona home alone for a second, but celebrating her eighteenth birthday was so important and he really wanted to take part in the planning of it. Besides, he knew his friends would be there for her and he wouldn't take that long. They had to get back to sword practice.

"Are you sure about being turned, Justin?" Jasmine asked while they were driving to the shopping center.

"Yeah. I think Fiona's mom would be a good choice, don't you?" Justin asked.

"Yeah. She wants to be your mom too," Caitlin said.

"That's another reason I want her to do it. I think we'll bond through the experience, and I really care for her. I mean, I thought she was my aunt and that she and my uncle were so cool. I always cared about them and wished Fiona and I could get in touch with them and thank them for everything."

"Okay. I think she's a good choice too," Jasmine said.

Arman was quiet. He couldn't quit thinking about Fiona.

Caitlin sighed. "Levka and the others will take care of Fiona."

"You really care about her, don't you?" Justin asked.

"Yeah. It's like we're connected."

"Then you'll have to turn her," Justin said.

"If she wants me to do it, I will, but she has to want it." Arman wasn't sure that she wanted to do it.

Then Caitlin changed the subject as they arrived at the shopping center. "Okay, balloons, party hats, strobe lights, a fog machine, music for a DJ party? What do you think? Fiona isn't going to be going to a prom night at a high school, so maybe a dance party?"

"Yeah, she would love that," Justin said. "Her favorite colors are blue and green."

"What would she like as gifts?" Jasmine asked. "We can have a cake made at this store and return in an hour."

They went inside a bakery and Justin said, "Oh, she would love this topper: 18 and Adultish with the crown on the 18 and the butterfly sitting on the crown. It's perfect. And she loves the water, so an ocean scene with the mermaid sitting on the rock?"

"That would cover the blue and green she loves," Caitlin said. "I love the topper too. And the ocean scene is beautiful."

They all looked at Arman. He smiled. "Yeah, that looks great."

They ordered a cake that could serve up to thirty people.

"Chocolate cake," Justin said. "That's her favorite."

Arman was glad that Justin was here because he knew so much about his sister! "Gifts, then?"

They bought her books, clothes, some games that they could

all play, puzzles. They really needed to have some fun things to do once they were no longer worried about Tobias coming for Fiona.

"Do you think he'll come for her tomorrow?" Justin asked as they dropped back by the bakery to pick up the cake after shopping for presents.

"I believe so," Arman said. "He went after Fiona's dad, turned her mom, Regina took her hostage, and then introduced Tobias to her. So yeah, I figure they will try to get to her tomorrow night. Or even before. So we have to make sure Fiona is being watched at all times."

Justin sighed. "Well, that's why I have to make sure I'm a vampire then. Tobias won't expect it."

"You know you'll be newly turned," Jasmine said.

"Yeah, the whole business with the fangs coming down can be problematic," Caitlin said.

"But at least you can vanish and reappear in a different place," Justin said, getting into the van with the others.

"Right. That would help you to get out of his path if Tobias came after you, and that could give someone else the chance to fight him," Caitlin said. "You're getting pretty good with a sword too. You have a really powerful swing."

"That's for sure," Jasmine said. "You absolutely were wearing me down and no vampire has ever fought me with that much power."

Justin beamed.

Arman smiled. He figured Justin would make a powerful fighter someday when his fighting skills were further honed.

"You need to turn my sister," Justin repeated to Arman. "She'll have more abilities, be safer, and the rest of the family will all be vampires as well."

Justin had a valid point. But it was still completely up to Fiona as to what she wanted to do.

18

"Tell me about yourself, uhm, uh, Dad?" Fiona was going to have to get used to calling her parents mom and dad. She wanted to. "My foster mother said you were CIA or something, but I guess that was a cover for why you weren't able to see us and had no address. Justin and I wanted to thank you for all the gifts you had given us over the years."

"That's the story we gave them. We could have wiped their minds of even knowing about us, but we had to make sure they used the money to take care of the two of you," her dad said. "Even though Justin wasn't our son, we wanted the two of you to be brother and sister growing up, and to do that, we needed to give both of you equal funds to take care of you."

"I appreciate that you did. His dad had problems."

"We didn't know that until we learned they had died and then we were on the search for where you had gone to. We knew Justin was away at college. We were paying for his tuition," her dad said. "Thankfully, Shelly and Michail came to his rescue so that Regina and Tobias didn't eliminate him too."

Great. Fiona finally had confirmation that Shelly and

Michail weren't bad guys. Though she thought it was odd that they didn't greet each other when they first arrived, like they had been fast friends. All her friends seemed friendlier to her parents than Shelly and Michail had been. They were smiling, a little standoffish, but maybe that was because they already knew each other and didn't need an introduction.

Ruric had slipped away, she realized, but then he returned with a platter of chocolate chip cookies. "Who wants dessert? It's not like the fancy pies Chef makes us, but we had the ingredients and it's the only dessert I know how to make."

"Oh, I love chocolate chip cookies. And double the chocolate chips. These are great." Fiona took three of them. "It's like an early birthday treat."

Ruric smiled. Everyone else grabbed a couple and Stasio made black tea to drink with the cookies.

"I'll clean up the dishes after we eat dessert." Fiona had planned to because the guys had all made the meal.

"We'll help," Ruric said.

And that was just what happened. After tea and cookies, they all had a soap suds party in the kitchen, cleaning dishes. Now this was fun.

"I WANT YOU TO TURN ME," Justin said to Arman on the trip back to the estate in the van, surprising the hell out of him.

He thought Bea was going to turn him.

"You don't want Bea to do it?"

"I want to do it now. Before we have the next sword practice. The sooner I can be changed, the sooner I can train as a vampire and not be so new at it."

"Well, alright, if you're sure."

"I am. How do we do this?"

"I can bite your wrist, and when your fangs come down, you can bite mine and it will be done. Unless you want to ask Fiona if you're alright with me changing you."

"Nope. It's my decision."

"Alright then. No changing your mind after it's done."

"Right. Got it." Then Justin rolled up his sleeve and offered his arm to Arman.

Caitlin and Jasmine were quiet. Arman just hoped he was doing the right thing by Justin. Arman extended his canines and Jasmine pulled over into a parking lot to make the exchange go more smoothly. If he did it right, Justin wouldn't feel any pain, just pleasure. He just hoped that Fiona wouldn't be pissed off at him for doing this to her brother.

Then he bit into him and glanced up to see Justin's eyes closed. Arman sucked on Justin blood, and then he sealed the bite. "My part is done."

Justin opened his eyes. "What? That was it?"

"You need to concentrate on extending your canines," Arman said.

They waited for what seemed like forever while Justin was frowning, trying to do something with his teeth. Then suddenly his eyes widened, and he smiled, showing off his extended canines. They were baby teeth compared to what they would be when he really got used to releasing them.

"Now?" Justin asked.

Arman pulled up his sleeve. "Drink some of my blood. I'll tell you when to stop and you stop. You'll have to get some control over it. You can have blood from the fridge when we return to the estate if you need more."

Justin eyed the blood pulsing in Arman's veins in his wrist. "I hear your heart beating. Jasmine's and Caitlin's too." Then he looked up at Arman. "Are...are you ready?"

Arman smiled. "Yeah, I am. Go ahead. You're halfway there."

Then Justin leaned over and licked Arman's wrist. His warm tongue tickled Arman's skin and he wanted to laugh. Then Justin sank his baby fangs into Arman's wrist, and he began to suck his blood. After Arman felt he'd had enough, he said, "Okay, that's it. There's more at home if you need it."

Justin hesitated, but then he released Arman.

"Lick the wound and it will seal it so there's no blood dripping from the wound. It will heal quickly," Arman said.

Justin licked the wound and stared at the bite marks that he had made and how they appeared to begin to fade.

Caitlin handed Justin a tissue. "You need to make sure you don't have any blood on your lips after you've had blood to drink."

But Justin just licked it off.

"Do you feel any differently?" Arman asked Justin. He hoped he felt only good things.

"Everything is so loud," Justin said.

"Welcome to our world," Jasmine said, starting up the van and heading home again.

"It's going to take some time to get used to it," Caitlin said.

"I'm trying to vanish. It's not working." Suddenly Justin was floating on the ceiling of the van.

"Woah, put your seatbelt on, dude," Arman said.

Justin laughed. "How do I get down from here?"

Trying not to show how amused he was, afraid he might offend Justin, Arman watched as Justin hung around the ceiling, his arms and legs outstretched as if he were flying, except he was just stationary. "Imagine yourself descending and then once your feet are on the floor of the van, sit, and strap yourself in."

They were nearly home when Justin fell off the ceiling onto the bench seat. "I did it. Not exactly like I wanted to, but wow, what a rush."

"You'll just need to practice. Maybe over your bed so you can land on the mattress and not hurt yourself."

Justin laughed. "I'll have to try that. I thought...well, I thought I would be able to have a lot more control over my vampire powers than this, come a fight tomorrow."

"You'll get it," Caitlin said. "Suddenly, it will just happen. Just keep practicing."

"I can't wait to try it out while we are fighting. Maybe I'll get it right then," Justin said.

"We'll practice together. I can hold your hand, or anyone else will and then that way you can't fly off and hurt yourself," Jasmine said.

"Thanks." Justin sounded relieved.

Then they finally arrived home and Arman really, really hoped Fiona wouldn't be mad at him for turning her brother.

FIONA HEARD the party planners return. She was curious as to what they came up with for the birthday party. She would be thrilled no matter what it was because it was so much better being with her friends here than at Regina's home with Tobias. But she was still worried about what was going to happen as far as the blood moon went.

But when she saw Arman, she smiled and felt so happy. There was just something about him that lit up her whole world. She thought he looked worried, though he gave her a small smile.

Justin looked like he was eager to tell her what they had gotten her for her birthday. She hadn't expected her brother to suddenly vanish. Her gaze riveted to Arman, right before he pulled her into his arms. "He insisted. I asked him if he was certain."

"You...you bit him."

"Yeah, I'm sorry. He said he didn't want me to ask you if you were alright with it," Arman said.

"No, no, it's his decision to make." In a way Fiona felt relieved that he had been turned by Arman. She trusted Arman, and her brother appeared so happy she was glad they'd done it. But then she realized he hadn't reappeared. "Justin?"

"I'm right here," Justin said, and reappeared right next to her, grinning. "Man, I love this." He gave her a hug. "Are you alright with this? That I'm now a vampire?" He showed his small canines. "And that Arman was the one who changed me?"

"Yes, to both. I think you will be better off as one in fights, or just to fit in more with family." She meant as far as her parents went since they were vampires now. She couldn't believe he had asked Arman to change him, but would it help in a fight with vampires? "Let's go practice sword fighting. We need to see what you can do with your vampire skills when it comes to fighting vampires now."

"I'm all for that." Her brother looked so eager and happy.

She was glad he was one of them now. She glanced at her mother, but she was only smiling, and she didn't seem to mind that Arman had turned Justin instead.

Then they all went to the grassy lawn to practice swordsmanship.

Fiona was total distracted, knowing she needed to concentrate on fighting Arman, but instead her attention was diverted to watching Justin fight with Jasmine. Fiona hoped Stasio wouldn't be upset about Jasmine teaching Justin. But she also figured that since Jasmine did this kind of work for a living, she would make for a really good teacher. And she was.

Justin was fighting her sword to sword then when Jasmine struck again trying to knock his sword from his hand. She did and sent it flying. But then before she could attack him when he was defenseless, he vanished. Fiona smiled. Now that was a great maneuver!

Suddenly, his sword disappeared, and he reappeared. Jasmine had been watching to see if Justin went for his sword and once he showed up, she immediately struck his sword with her own, but he held onto it more firmly and fought back. She glanced at Arman, and he was smiling.

"It looks like he's going to do well with his new skills. I don't think I've ever seen a newly turned vampire who has so much fun with his new abilities," Arman said.

Fiona smiled. "Yeah, I didn't think he would either. Despite how we grew up in such a dysfunctional family, he was always good-natured and fun-loving."

"He sure seems that way. I'm so glad he has taken this so well," Arman said. "Do you want to practice?"

Fiona laughed. "Sure." Then they started to playfight, and she was thinking it would be fun if she could vanish like her brother had done. But she wasn't interested in the blood thing.

She was just as strong as Arman when connecting with his sword and she assumed it was because she was a huntress. She saw her mother and father practicing their sword fighting and she was fascinated to see how they fought each other. Both were excellent fighters.

Arman touched her shoulder, and she hadn't realized he'd gotten that close. "Sorry," she said. "I was just curious how my parents were at fighting."

"Because you're worried about them."

"Yes. If Tobias can control my mom, that would be bad news." Fiona frowned at Arman. "Is that why you turned Justin instead of letting my mom do it?"

"I had thought of it, but the main reason was that Justin

didn't want to wait. He asked me and he wanted to do it then, before we did weapons training again."

"I'm glad you did it. Okay, we're going to do this." She started fighting Arman again, but then Jasmine switched out with him, and Arman put Justin through his paces.

Jasmine was smiling as she fought Fiona. "Your brother is a character. I'm so glad that he is one of us now. He's doing really great fighting as a vampire now. So much better than when he was solely a human. He has got our strength now and that's good."

"Exactly." Fiona was glad and was hoping that would mean that he would stay safe. After fighting Jasmine for a while, her mother came over to battle it out with Fiona. "You were alright with Arman turning Justin instead of you, aren't you?"

"Yes. After I'd offered, I had realized if Tobias ends up here, he could control me and force me to control your brother. Your father would have done the deed instead."

Fiona's mother was an excellent swordswoman. She kept Fiona on her toes. Unlike when Fiona was fighting Arman, she found her mother was tricky. She kept vanishing and coming in for another attack. Which was great! It helped Fiona learn how to fight vampires who used their abilities to try and take the advantage. But Fiona was listening hard, and she could hear her mother's heartbeat just as she reappeared behind her or to her side. Fiona wasn't used to being able to use her hearing in that way—to really concentrate on the sounds around her, blocking out the sounds of the fighting all around her—to protect herself.

She was doing really well fighting a vampire when she didn't have their abilities, she thought. Her father came to take her mother's place, but Fiona was getting tired by now. "Did you ask Mom to turn you?" She knew that her mother had done so to protect him from Tobias, but had she just turned him in a hurry, and he hadn't really had any choice?

He smiled at her. "We discussed it, but we didn't have a lot of time to make a decision. Tobias was trying to get Bea to bring me to him. She was fighting his telepathic suggestion. We found a home for you, then we moved to Germany, any place to get free of Tobias's control. We continued to travel, to evade him, while we continued to pay for you and for Justin as you grew up. We couldn't reach you fast enough once your foster parents had died. We traveled through Scotland, learned what Arman and his friends had done, and I was able to connect with him in a dream."

"Did you know I had run into Arman at the Dallas mall two years earlier?"

"Yeah. I had something to do with that. I knew he had dreams like I do, like you do. I knew he was a vampire and he helped hunters and humans who were in need. I knew he and his friends would help you if he ever learned of you and you became Tobias's next target."

"How did you have something to do with me running into Arman?" She had always wondered how she had been so clumsy to have spilled her soda on him. She swore she had tripped over her own feet, and she wasn't normally like that.

Her father struck her sword, but he was a lot easier on her than Arman or her mother was. "I had to get you to make a connection with him. I couldn't have spoken for you, but when he offered to take you to lunch, I wanted to step in and tell you to do it."

"I was so embarrassed. I was with my brother there, and I'm sure he wouldn't have liked that I'd just met some guy I didn't know, spilled soda all over him, and then had lunch with him."

Her dad smiled at her, and he quit fighting her to talk.

Then Fiona frowned. "How did you know he had dreams like you?" She needed to learn what her father could do with his dreams and what she could do with hers.

"You feel it. You share them. You know. You had dreams of him."

"Okay, true. So you had dreams with him?"

"I could see into his dreams. I saw into yours. When you were just a toddler, your mom and I had to leave Dallas because Tobias had turned your mother in an attempt to control her so that she would help him use me. But she turned me instead."

"How did you end up with the dreaming ability?"

"I was born with it, just like you were, but it takes time before you even realize you have it. And it does grow on you."

Did that mean if Fiona had a child, he or she would have the same ability and then they would have to deal with rogues like Regina and Tobias trying to take control of her child? "What can I do with it?"

"My grandmother had the same ability. For her, she was able to change nightmares into comedy or something pleasant and an agreeable dream into a nightmare."

"For whom? Could she do it with anyone?"

"For anyone. I have the same abilities. But I also can suggest changes in someone's behavior."

"Like telling Arman I needed help."

"Exactly. I couldn't force him to do it. He had to make his own decision whether to help you, but having already met you earlier and liking you, and because he and his companions were known to help people in need, he was the perfect candidate for the job. I knew if anyone could rescue you, it was him and his friends. Since that day when you had first met him, their little vampire pack had gained a couple of new members who would only be a help in getting you to safety and keeping you safe until your mother and I could arrive."

"But if Tobias arrives here, then he could control Mom and make her fight us too." It was hard to believe her mother could be forced to hurt Fiona, but for Tobias to get his way, he would do anything that gave him the advantage.

"Yes. We need to protect her as much as we need to protect you. I couldn't leave her on her own in another country for fear Tobias would get to her," Fiona's father said.

"Okay, I understand. So what happens when the blood moon is here? I'm already having the dreams and some control over them. What changes?" she asked.

"You'll be able to get into anyone's dreams whether you're sleeping or not, targeting someone, or just 'listening' in. You can tell them to do something you need them to accomplish, a suggestion that is so real that when they wake, they'll know they have to do it."

"Kind of like a vampiric suggestion, or command of a human."

"Right, but you can do it with a vampire."

"Oh, sure. I've done that with my friends."

Her father smiled.

"I didn't give them nightmares."

"But you can. And when you turn eighteen, you'll even be able to give someone like Regina or Tobias nightmares or suggestions."

"Why couldn't *you* do that with them?"

"I hadn't had my full abilities yet, and Tobias was after me, trying to use Bea against me. We had to leave. But I don't know if you'll have the same abilities as me."

"When did you get your abilities?"

"I was twenty-five and it was during the wolf moon."

Fiona sighed. "So if Tobias comes here, what are you going to do with Mom?"

"As much as I hate to do it, but she also agrees, we'll have to lock her up so he can't get to her easily."

"And we'll have a couple of people post guards. Uhm, how do you feel about Arman turning Justin?"

"It was a good call. He's our son too. We feel that with all of our hearts, and we want him to continue to be part of our lives. It would have been too risky for him to fight ruthless vampires like Tobias without being one of us," her father said. "It's your choice, but we would feel better if you were also one of us."

19

That night, Arman and the others went swimming, before the big day. "Are you worried about tomorrow, Fiona?"

"Yeah, but I'm looking forward to the birthday party too." She swam around Arman and then he pulled her into his arms. She told him what her dad said about his abilities and what she might be able to do once she turned eighteen.

"Have you been able to see any of Shelly or her brother's dreams?" Arman asked. They were inside the house, not interested in swimming.

"No. I keep trying at night, but I'm not able to."

"When were you born? I mean, the hour of your birth?" Arman asked.

"One in the morning."

"Hmm, so then if this is all true, you'll actually have your abilities shortly after the bewitching hour."

"Yeah. I was thinking just sometime tomorrow, but I should have it while we're sleeping. I'll try to see what I can do with everyone for fun."

Arman said to all their friends and her brother and parents,

"Since Fiona was born at one in the morning, we need to have a couple of us guard her at all times."

Everyone agreed.

"And my mom too, in case Tobias ends up here and tries to control her," Fiona said.

"Absolutely," Levka said. "We have about thirty people at our disposal who were glad we helped them to overthrow the League here. They're here and you'll see one or two of them occasionally, but they're really trying to be inconspicuous and will come to our aid if we need them. Because we have a long night and day ahead of us, I suggest we have dinner, and retire to bed, except for those pulling guard duty."

Everyone began getting out of the pool and grabbing towels. Then Arman took Fiona in his arms and transported her to their bedroom. She smiled at him. "I will never get used to you doing that to me."

"Which is why you need to be one of us. I can't bear the thought of potentially losing you tomorrow."

She put her hands on his shoulders and kissed him. "Which is why you're going to turn me."

He was shocked and his expression revealed how much so. And he was speechless.

"Okay, look, I see what my brother can do and how happy he is to have all these new feats. Everyone in my family is a vampire now. I'll feel like everyone will always have to watch out for me because I won't be as strong as you. I...I want to be with you and for that reason alone, I want to be a vampire also. Who knows? Maybe if Tobias comes for me, he'll be so shocked that I'm one too now, we'll be able to catch him off-guard and take him down."

Arman wanted to do this with her. He wanted her in his life not for just a brief time, but for a vampire's long life. If they were going to do this, before her eighteenth birthday would be preferable.

"But we don't tell anyone."

He frowned. "Do you think your parents would object?"

"No. Dad said he wants me to be a vampire too. I just think it would be beneficial if no one knew...unless I have to deal with Tobias or his minions."

"I wouldn't keep a secret like that from my friends. Our friends. If you want to wait to tell your parents later, that's fine."

She sighed. "Yes and not Shelly and Michail either."

He rubbed her arms. "You must have a reason that you want to keep this secret from the others."

"I...I don't trust Shelly and Michail. Don't ask me why. It's just something instinctual. Did you notice they never practice fight with us? They don't swim with us either. They eat with us, but they're...distant. They did rescue my brother, but maybe they had an ulterior motive. What if Tobias sent them to learn where you were staying? What if he told them to pick up my brother and bring him here as a show of how they are on our side? They said they were friends of Tobias, and of my parents. But what if they made contact with my parents for the same dark purpose? To get us all here in one place where Tobias and his people could make their move? What if my parents think Shelly and Michail are friends when they really aren't?" Fiona asked.

"I agree. Though your parents don't seem to interact with them much."

"True. So bite me and let's do this," Fiona said.

"I'm not going to ask if you're sure because I know you are." He leaned down and kissed her. His hand swept through her hair and then he rested his forehead against hers for a moment. "I love you."

She pulled him into her arms and gave him a warm hug. "I

love you too from the moment I christened you with a cup of sticky, carbonated soda. You were the hottest guy I had ever run into, with the help of my father, I might add."

"What?"

"Yeah, he said it was not an accident."

"I will have to thank him for that." Then before she worried about the next step, Arman pushed the hair away from Fiona's neck and she offered it to him like a human who was under a vampire's charm would do. Only she was a huntress, and she couldn't be charmed in that manner. Which was just the way he wanted it. Her choice entirely.

He licked, she chuckled, and he extended his canines, not showing them to her for fear of making her afraid of him and sank his teeth into her neck. He drank from her blood and then he sealed the bite marks. He kissed her again, waiting for her canines to extend, stroking her tongue with his until he felt her canines start to grow. He realized since she would have so little control over them to begin with, they would probably extend every time they were kissing.

Levka said telepathically, *"What is taking you so long? We're waiting on you for dinner, Arman. You and Fiona."*

"Coming." Arman didn't want to say anything more than that. Not when they were trying to complete the blood bonding. "Do you want to bite my wrist or neck?"

Fiona looked a little dazed. "Hmm."

"If you're afraid to bite me, I can bite my own wrist and you can drink my blood that way." He hoped she didn't back out on him now, worried about going through with it. Though if she did, they could try later. Maybe her teeth would extend given time.

She licked his neck. That tickled, which was why she probably had laughed earlier when he had done that to her. But she didn't bite.

"Arman?" Levka persisted. Maybe he was worried about them.

"I don't mean to rush you, but Levka is worried about us not joining them for dinner." Arman bit into his arm and offered his blood to her. "My sleeve will cover the teeth marks and then we can keep the secret from everyone. If you bit my neck, everyone would see it."

She was eyeing his blood.

"You have to hurry, or the wound will heal enough that the blood will be gone, though I'll still have the puncture marks for a while."

She took his arm and hesitantly drank his blood, but then really had a taste for it. Though he was glad she was alright with drinking his blood, he finally had to stop her. "Okay, that's enough for you for now. You can drink some more from a cup when you need more. Let's join the others. I'll hold onto you, but you try and take us down to the bottom of the stairs, not to the dining room in case you land in the wrong place."

"We did it." She was so bright eyed when she gazed up at him, full of wonder and she appeared happy that they had done it.

"Yes, and Levka will be up here momentarily if we don't go downstairs."

She wrapped her arms around Arman. "How do I do it?"

"Imagine you're at the bottom of the stairs."

The next thing he knew they were at the bottom of the stairs...in the swimming pool.

"Ohmigod," she said, both of them standing in warm water up to their waists.

He laughed. He couldn't help himself. This was going to be interesting. He told Levka, *"I turned Fiona. We're in the swimming pool again. As soon as we get changed again, we'll be down. You can tell our friends, no one else."*

"Not even Fiona's parents or brother?"

"Not yet." Then Arman said to Fiona, "Okay, take us to our bedroom."

"Are you sure?"

"Yes. The more practice you have, the better you'll get at it."

"Thanks, Arman." Then she tried this time and got the bedroom right.

They hurried to change, but before they went downstairs, she gave him a hug and a kiss. "Thanks for understanding."

"I have to admit I hadn't expected to be standing in the pool." He chuckled again. But this time, he took hold of her and transported them to the dining room. They took their usual seats while everyone was passing around a casserole dish of lasagna and a platter of garlic toast. Several glanced in their direction and Arman figured they were curious about what was going on.

Arman wondered if Levka had told their friends what had happened.

Then Levka said to Arman, *"We'll tell our friends after dinner, since you don't want to mention it to the others and we don't want to accidentally give away the secret."*

"Thanks, Levka."

"So how is the guard schedule going to work?" Michail asked.

"We have Scottish friends who will be responsible for guard duty. The rest of us will just get our sleep unless something happens that requires our action," Levka said.

Jasmine finally said to Arman, *"Did you turn Fiona?"*

"Yes, but we were going to keep it just among ourselves, and no one else. Not Fiona's family even."

"And you aren't going to tell Shelly and Michail either, right?" Jasmine asked.

"Right." Arman saw Jasmine lean over and kiss Stasio and she

squeezed his hand. She knew she was telling him what was going on, but making sure he didn't give away the secret.

Levka probably had already told Caitlin. Arman had to tell Ruric then, not wanting him to be left out in the cold.

Ruric toasted to Fiona, "May your birthday tomorrow be the best ever."

Arman had been afraid he'd mention her being turned, so he was glad he hadn't said anything about that.

"Have you discussed being turned again?" Michail said. "I really believe it would be in your best interest, Fiona. Especially since your brother and parents are already turned."

"No. I don't believe it would help me. Maybe later, but it would probably take me too long to use any vampiric abilities to my advantage," Fiona said.

"Fiona's right," Caitlin said. "Some of these abilities took me months to really get used to and some I still haven't been able to master."

"I don't know," Justin said. "I still think you would have an advantage against rogue vampires if you're one of them. Or maybe not an advantage, but at least more on an equal footing."

"If I had mastered the abilities. If I hadn't, it could prove disastrous."

Arman hoped Fiona really didn't feel that way because of the mistake she'd made in transporting them to the pool.

She leaned over and kissed his cheek as if reassuring him she was fine with it all.

"So what time were you really born?" Shelly asked.

"One in the afternoon," Fiona's father said.

"Yes, I kept thinking I would have Fiona. I had gone in at eight in the evening and then it was hours and hours and hours before she was born. I actually went home and walked for a while, returned to the hospital and walked some more. And then finally at one in the afternoon, she was there. Well, ten after one to be precise," Fiona's mother said.

Had Fiona mixed up the hour of her birth or were her parents trying to pretend she was born later so that she would have the full advantage of her dream abilities before anyone knew she had them?

If so, that was a great ploy.

Arman was trying not to glance at Fiona too much, hoping she was able to keep her fangs sheathed or not while she was eating. He hoped she would have an easier time of it than Caitlin had.

"So should we have the birthday party at ten after one then?" Fiona asked, sounding happy to do it.

"Absolutely," her mother said. "We got you a couple of gifts too."

Fiona smiled. "Thanks, Mom."

They visited after dinner, but then everyone was eager to go to bed to be ready for the day ahead of them. Especially since Arman and his friends knew that Fiona's abilities would most likely appear at one in the morning.

Everyone retired to their rooms and Fiona and Arman settled in bed together. They snuggled together. He was worried about her, but with their extra guards and everyone else here who would protect her, he felt pretty certain Fiona would be okay.

She smiled and kissed him. "We'll be fine."

He sure hoped so, though he couldn't help but think about the dream he'd had and that he couldn't find Fiona, then the fighting had started. When did that actually happen? All he knew was that it was dark out when he found Fiona was missing from the bed.

FIONA WAS TORN between wanting to sleep before she might end up in a fight against Tobias and his minions, practicing using her vampire skills, practicing sword fighting some more, or trying to infiltrate her friends' dreams. Still, she was tired, and while she was cuddling with Arman, she fell into a sound sleep.

Fiona felt she was drifting into the wispy clouds, the dark sky filled with twinkling stars, the full moon taking on a reddish cast. The blood moon! It was huge, taking up most of the sky, beautiful, amazing and she felt connected to it all at once.

Fiona "saw" Levka fighting Arman in sword practice and Caitlin exposing her small canines in a grin. Fiona watched as her brother floated below the van's ceiling as he tested out his vampiric abilities. She saw her mother biting her father and him biting her back, then hand-in-hand, running for their lives. Ruric came into view, being hunted by a man and a woman dressed in black leather, both armed with swords, hunters? Vampire hunters? She didn't know, but she made them stop, toss their swords, and begin to kiss each other. Ruric glanced back at them, raised his brows, but then he vanished, free of the hunters' pursuit. Jasmine was after a hunter, but lost him, and saved a little girl from harm, returning her to her human parents. Stasio was reading one of his books on...War Tactics.

Then she saw Shelly and Michail walking through the gardens. She drew closer to listen in.

"They're here, waiting for the signal," Shelly said.

"I hope they have enough of a force to overwhelm about forty vampires, well, and one huntress," Michail said.

"They won't approach until it's one-ten in the afternoon, the time when Fiona turns eighteen."

Fiona knew not to trust them! Her instincts were often on the mark. She was so angry, she envisioned a king cobra the size of a man biting at Michail, and a sinkhole swallowing up Shelly. Not that Fiona could actually make them dream of those things, but suddenly, both were crying out and Fiona nearly fell to the ground. She hadn't been dreaming that part. She was really floating up in the clouds and spying on Michail and Shelly! Well, giving them nightmares while they were awake, terrorizing them.

She had to return to tell the others that she had learned of their deceitfulness, that Tobias and his people were here, waiting to attack them.

Suddenly, Tobias was next to Shelly and Michail, shaking Shelly first. "Snap out of it. Fiona's got her powers already, damn it. It's after one in the morning. Her mother lied to you about Fiona's actual birth time."

But Shelly couldn't shake loose of the feeling that she was sinking into the sinkhole, and it was closing around her. Tobias shook Michail then, trying to get him to listen to him. "Get ahold of yourself, man."

Boy, was Tobias pissed.

Fiona was going to call out to Arman and their friends telepathically when Tobias saw her. Crap! She tried to vanish, but she couldn't. The next thing she knew, she was trying to fly out of Tobias's reach. He knew now she was a vampire, no longer just a huntress. Thank God, she also had her sword belted at her waist. Still, she needed to alert the others because more of Tobias's vampires were here, and they could be a threat to her friends and family.

But she realized she couldn't send them a warning, not while she was trying to evade the powerful vampire.

20

Arman woke. He wasn't sure why, then he realized Fiona was no longer in bed with him. He immediately alerted his friends, their guards, and Fiona's family, though he really didn't want Justin in the middle of all this, feeling he wasn't ready to fight vampires yet. Which really was the same for Fiona. He did not alert Shelly and Michail. *"The blood moon is out, Fiona's not here. It's after one in the morning."*

He threw on his clothes, grabbed his sword, and headed out of the room. Everyone was leaving their bedrooms at the same time, pulling on shirts or shoes, their swords sheathed at their waists.

"Did you check the bathroom?" Caitlin asked.

"Yes."

"The kitchen?" Ruric asked.

"No. But if this is anything like that dream or vision I had, Fiona is not in the mansion any longer," Arman said, then vanished and was in the gardens. *"Fiona!"*

Levka joined him. And then the others did. *"Spread out. Let us know if you find any trouble."*

Then they heard sword fighting in the herb gardens, and they all headed that way.

Arman couldn't believe it when he saw Shelly writhing on the ground in distress as if she'd been poisoned, and Michail was holding onto something, trying to keep it away from him, his arms outstretched, his face a ghastly mask of horror, but there was nothing in his grasp that Arman could see. But then he heard the sound of clanking steel again, and he hurried past the crazed vampires in search of the source of the fighting. *"Fiona!"*

All at once the gardens were filled with vampires, not Arman's friends, but strangers they didn't know. They were likewise armed and intent to fight, their expressions full of malevolence. Levka and the others began engaging them in combat, but Arman was still searching for Fiona, avoiding fighting anyone as much as possible so he could reach her more quickly. But a tall, slender vampire targeted him, and Arman quickly dispensed with him, furious beyond measure that anyone would try to thwart him from his mission.

Fiona cried out behind one of the greenhouses, and Arman instantly reappeared there and saw her fighting Tobias. Arman's heart beat triple time, fear for her and anger swamping him.

"You turned her, didn't you?" Tobias said, angry as hell. He whipped around to kill Arman. But Arman wasn't a new vampire.

Though Arman also knew that Tobias would realize he was the real threat to him.

Fiona was favoring her arm and Arman realized Tobias had cut her. He smelled her blood and wanted to end the vampire instantly, but he had to keep his head. Getting emotionally embroiled in a fight could be the death of him and he had to protect Fiona at all costs.

He swung his sword at Tobias and the vampire connected

with his, hitting it so hard, Arman's whole arm vibrated with the jolt. *"Tobias is here behind the greenhouse,"* he told his friends, suspecting the reason Fiona hadn't called out to them was because after being so newly turned, she couldn't manage telepathically communicating with them while fighting to save her life against the vicious vampire. *"Fiona's injured."*

"Coming," Caitlin and Jasmine said.

Arman knew they were all fighting. He could hear the sword fighting going on around the perimeter of the estate. But he also knew they needed more help here to protect Fiona. She was the real target.

"Regina's here," Arman said as she went straight for Fiona.

Fiona had been resting, holding her injured arm, in obvious pain. She wasn't healing as fast as he thought she should. But then Caitlin and Jasmine showed up and both took Regina on while he continued to fight Tobias. The next thing he knew, Clarissa, the Egyptian girl came out of nowhere and headed for Fiona.

"You don't want to mess with me," Fiona told Clarissa, her voice threatening. She swung her sword at Clarissa, but to swing well, Fiona needed the strength of both arms, but her injury was making her swing much weaker than when she'd practiced. She hated coming to the fight that she had to win, injured before she had barely begun.

"Or else, what? All I need to do is turn you and then you're mine," Clarissa said.

She was going to be in for a surprise when she realized Fiona was already a vampire. Fiona saw Arman glance in her direction, and she knew his worried look meant he feared for her when she wanted him to concentrate on the fight between him and Tobias. He couldn't safely risk watching her fight while battling Tobias.

Just like right now, she needed to watch out for Clarissa's powerful swing and not concern herself with how Arman was faring as much as she did worry about it. Clarissa purposely struck Fiona's sword with such power, Fiona lost her sword, and she swore under her breath.

Fiona disappeared—to her surprise and from the look on Clarissa's slack-jawed expression, Clarissa's too—and then reappeared where her sword had landed. Fiona grabbed it up, but Clarissa was attacking her with a vengeance, probably pissed off that someone from Fiona's court had turned her and Clarissa now didn't have the chance.

Fiona feared she wouldn't win this fight against the powerful teen vamp as hard as Clarissa was striking her sword and Fiona could only defend herself. She tried to control Clarissa's thoughts like it seemed she'd done with Shelly and Michail, but like she'd tried with Tobias, she wasn't able to. Maybe later, when she had better control of it. But not when she had a lot of distraction—like trying to keep herself alive while in a sword fight and she was newly trained at it.

She heard her brother shout off in the distance and she prayed he was alright. She worried about her mother, that Tobias might try to influence her to show up here too and force Fiona to fight her own mom. She wouldn't be able to do it.

Fiona thought about being a dragon, breathing fire, to wedge that fear into Clarissa's thoughts but only for a split second as Clarissa's thrusts were taking way too much of Fiona's focus. Her arm was hurting something fierce, a burning sensation growing. Blood dripping down her arm made her realize just how much she could smell blood now, and she noticed how Clarissa had glanced that way several times, as if she wanted a taste...or to drain her. More likely the latter.

But then Clarissa slammed her sword with such ferocity against Fiona's again, the impact sent her sword flying through the air. Before Fiona could vanish, Clarissa lunged and grabbed for Fiona's throat.

∼

Arman was still fighting Tobias, both slicing at each other, both trying to keep from being fatally cut. He couldn't help but glance in Fiona's direction though, worried for her. For the second time, she'd lost her sword as Clarissa had struck it so hard.

Arman wanted to destroy Tobias and go to Fiona's aid, but Caitlin suddenly left Jasmine to fight Regina on her own, and targeted Clarissa. Caitlin screened Fiona in fog, allowing her to escape Clarissa's wrath. Then Fiona could move from where she was last standing to a new location. Caitlin waved her hands in her witch's way and threw Clarissa over an ancient stone retaining wall and the vampire fell into the rosebushes.

Arman was glad for her witch's skills, which had improved with every passing day. Tobias struck again, and Arman countered the attack, but then Tobias vanished. Instantly, Arman was afraid Tobias had gone after Fiona! *"Where are you, Fiona?"* Arman called to her telepathically.

"In the greenhouse. I'm starting to heal. I can help fight again. I retrieved my sword."

"Tobias is coming for you." Arman joined her in the greenhouse, but she was alone, for now. *"Drink my blood. It'll help heal you faster."*

Before he could bite into his wrist to offer his blood, Fiona screamed, *"Behind you, Arman!"*

Arman whipped around and cut Tobias across the cheek. He

roared with pain and frustration, falling back, his eyes filled with hatred.

Fiona slipped around Tobias, slashed at him, and managed to slice his arm like he had done to her.

Tobias again cried out. "If you don't come willingly with me, I will have everyone here killed, including your brother and your parents," Tobias said to Fiona, his brown eyes darkened to black. He was still advancing on Arman, who was trying to get a good fatal strike in at the vampire.

Fiona was holding her sword up, stalking around Tobias, but he was listening to her movements and Arman knew if she tried to strike him, he would whip around and cut her again. He knew if Tobias couldn't use her powers, she would be useless to him, and he would prefer killing her so no one else could use them.

Outside the greenhouse, Jasmine and Caitlin were still fighting Regina and Clarissa when Arman heard Levka join the women. "You want to side with Tobias? You have made a fatal mistake."

"As if you can win," Clarissa said.

But in the next instant, Clarissa cried out, and Levka shouted, "Regina, you're next."

Arman knew he was calling out for Tobias to hear because Regina and Clarissa had been friends of his. Arman knew Levka did it to help rattle Tobias. But the vampire didn't seem to care. He wanted Fiona's ability and that's all that mattered to him.

Fiona was standing off to the side, plotting maybe when to make another strike at Tobias, while Arman was continually deflecting Tobias's slashes and thrusts, unable to switch to the offensive and knock him off kilter again. It reminded him of the trouble Fiona had been having with Clarissa, always defending, never being able to advance.

Suddenly, Fiona's brother appeared and sliced at Tobias's back, cutting him. Tobias growled with pain.

Arman had mixed feelings about it, not wanting her brother to be injured since he was so newly turned and so newly trained to sword fight.

Arman was trying to keep Tobias's attention on him, and not turn to strike at Justin.

Then Fiona's father rushed into the greenhouse. Now Arman was sure between them, they would be able to take Tobias down.

"You!" Tobias screamed out.

Through the greenhouse windows, Arman could see Jasmine and Levka fighting Regina. Caitlin was casting spells and he saw Regina fall once for no apparent reason.

Arman assumed Regina was as good a fighter as Tobias. He hoped Levka or his other friends would hurry up and help him with Tobias. Arman was wearing down. And Fiona's father wasn't using his sword on Tobias. Justin was waiting for a chance to strike at the vampire again. Arman hoped her father didn't feel that Arman needed to win the battle on his own for some honorable reason. He understood why Justin was holding back.

But suddenly, Tobias held up his sword like he was pointing to the ceiling of the glass greenhouse, and he angrily turned his head to glower at Fiona.

Had she infiltrated his mind? Commanded him to do that? Arman raised his brows. Had her father helped her? Arman immediately thrust his sword into Tobias's chest and hit his heart dead on. Justin struck Tobias in the side at the same time. The look of shock on Tobias's face would stick with Arman forever before the vampire disintegrated into ashes. All that remained was his black leather clothes in a crumpled pile on the greenhouse floor.

Arman glanced at the greenhouse window just as he saw Levka and Jasmine strike Regina from the front when Caitlin struck her from behind, and the vampire disintegrated like

Tobias had done, leaving skinny jeans, boots, a black leather jacket, and a black tunic shirt on the ground.

Levka rushed into the greenhouse to come to Fiona's aid.

"Too late," Arman said. "Fiona and her brother and father helped me to destroy Tobias."

But the fighting was going on still, and they had to help their friends. Arman said, "I'm giving Fiona some blood and I'll join you."

They all glanced at her. She looked pale and disheveled. Arman quickly bit into his arm and gave her his blood. She drank of it and looked like she felt better right away. He wanted her to return to their room, but she couldn't be alone. And no matter how many guards he sent to watch over her, he didn't feel she would be safe unless he was there with her.

"We're off to help the others," Levka said, and he, Fiona's father, and Justin left.

"Are you going to be alright, Fiona?" Arman asked the love of his life.

"Yes, let's go," Fiona said.

Caitlin and Jasmine were waiting for them outside of the greenhouse.

Fiona said to them, "Shelly and Michail were in league with Tobias. I heard them talking about it."

"Did you do something to them?" Arman asked, puzzled as to what the matter was with them.

"Michail is fighting a king cobra. Shelly can't get out of a sinkhole."

"Good. They deserved it I'm sure," Caitlin said.

They all hurried off in the direction of the sound of more fighting.

"Tobias came for me, and I couldn't concentrate on calling you, just on keeping him from cutting me in two. He was really angry that you had turned me," Fiona said to Arman.

"I was really angry he had cut you." Arman wondered where Fiona's mother was. Now with Tobias gone, he couldn't control her, but before that? He could have.

When they reached where Shelly and Michail were, they were gone, only their clothes and piles of ash were left behind.

"I didn't do it," Fiona said. "I...I don't think I did."

Jasmine shook her head. "I would have terminated both of them for setting us all up."

Then Fiona saw her mother fighting a vampire and Fiona flew to where she was and struck the vampire in the shoulder. Her mother hit the vampire in the heart, and he disintegrated in the air, his clothes dropping to the ground.

Arman soon was engaged with another vampire and then he helped Fiona's father fight another one before Fiona had to fight anyone else. Arman and Nathaniel quickly dispensed with the vampire her father had been fighting.

"You killed Tobias, didn't you, Arman?" Fiona's mother said.

"Yes. Tobias is dead. So are Regina and Clarissa." As soon as Arman spoke the words, the sword fighting that had been going on stopped.

The Scottish vampires who were there to help Levka and his friends all shouted out with cheers.

Ruric and Stasio joined Levka and the others. Ruric said, "As soon as you said Tobias, Regina, and Clarissa were dead, the vampires we were fighting vanished."

"They might have been turned by one of the three of the vampires and now they've been set free," Arman said. "They no longer have a leader among them."

Bea said, "That's how I feel. I've been set free of Tobias's control. While he was concentrating on fighting, he had no control over me. That's the only reason I was able to battle it out with his minions. Even so, I didn't want to go anywhere near where Fiona was, in case he could control me if I had gotten too close to him." Then she frowned at Fiona and took her into her arms. "You're injured."

"It'll heal up quickly," Fiona said.

They noticed some of the vampires who were their friends and there to safeguard them were wandering through the gardens and Arman knew they were making sure none of Tobias's people were still hanging around. Without a leader, they would have to either find another clan or pack to belong to or start their own with new leadership. But they most likely would return to the States.

They glanced up at the sky and marveled at the beauty of the blood red moon.

"I know I'm now eighteen, and we could celebrate my birthday, but would anyone mind if we wait until later in the morning?" Fiona asked.

"No, get your rest," her mother said, giving her a gentle hug.

Her father hugged her too. "You did well for your first time as a vampire fighting for your life. And I saw what you did to Shelly and Michail."

"I didn't kill Shelly and Michail, did I?"

"No. But you put them in a state of terror so they couldn't fight any of us. I put them out of their misery," her father said. "They hadn't planned to let Tobias take you for your powers. They planned to do it instead. They had no idea that you had already turned eighteen, had your full powers, and had been turned by Arman. It was a good thing that you kept the secret from them."

"I didn't trust them," Fiona said. "Sorry that we didn't share Arman's turning me with you and Mom."

"No problem. All that matters was that you are safe at the end of all this."

"Did you use your abilities on anyone?" Fiona asked her father.

"I saw you struggling to do something to Tobias. I was able to 'see' what you were doing and then I was able to boost your ability. It's something I've never been able to do with anyone before. It was amazing. He was a powerful vampire. I'm not sure I could have done it on my own either." Her father smiled down at her.

She threw her arms around her dad and hugged him. "I felt it. A sudden surge of energy and then Tobias reacted like I'd hoped for. Thanks for helping me. We made a great team."

Her mom just smiled at them, looking happy that Fiona and her father could connect with each other using their dream skills to help Arman take down the powerful vampire.

"Wow, the two of you can go with me anytime when I have to take down a rogue vampire," Jasmine said.

No way did Arman want Fiona to go anywhere to fight vampires again. Not until she was truly proficient with her sword fighting skills, vampire abilities, and her dream power.

Jasmine's hunter brother, Brett, Stasio's hunter cousins Llewellyn, Cadfael, and his vampire cousin, Gareth, all joined them from battle and sheathed their swords, greeting the others.

"That was a battle worth fighting," Llewellyn said.

"Aye," Cadfael said. "We are glad you called on us to help out. The vampires were no match for us, but we did get in a wee bit of practice."

Gareth laughed. "I had to help you fight three of the bastards they were so tough."

Cadfael and Llewellyn smiled.

"I do admit it helps sometimes to have a vampire aid us when he has your skills, brother," Llewellyn said to Gareth.

Gareth looked at Cadfael, waiting for his brother to agree.

"Aye, aye, I agree with Llewellyn, but dinna let it go to your head, wee brother," Cadfael said.

Gareth smiled, looking like he was on top of the world that

his brothers would admit his being a vampire, through no fault of his own, had helped them in their battle against the rogues.

Brett gave his sister a hug. "I'm glad to see you doing well."

"And you, dear brother." Jasmine hugged him back.

Arman, Fiona, and the rest of the group all walked back to the mansion while the others who had been there to help fight the threat made sure they'd gone after everyone. Arman and their friends could have just reappeared inside the building, but sometimes after a fight with the adrenaline flooding their blood, they needed to walk it off a bit.

"Happy birthday, darling daughter," Fiona's mom said as they entered the mansion.

"Happy birthday, little one," her dad said, heading up the stairs with Fiona's mom.

Justin gave her a hug too.

"You did great," Fiona said. "I was struggling to use my abilities and here you were, a newly turned vampire, attacking an ancient vampire, Justin."

Justin sighed. "That was the best birthday present I could give you."

"For sure."

Arman agreed. Her brother had helped to give her the gift of life.

Everyone echoed the happy birthday sentiments and retired to their rooms. Once Arman and Fiona returned to theirs, he checked Fiona's wound, but it was healing already and didn't even need a bandage. Then they joined each other in bed.

"Why did you leave me?" he asked, cuddling her in his arms. He was thinking he would have to tie her wrist to his so she wouldn't just vanish like that if it had to do with her not being able to control her vampire abilities to vanish and reappear in other places.

"I was visiting everyone's dreams and the next thing I knew, I was floating among the clouds, but that part had been real."

"As a vampire. Outside."

"Yes. Thankfully, I had taken a real sword with me in what I thought was just a dream. I was drawn to the blood moon. I think I was out there all along, intercepting dreams. But then I overheard Shelly and Michail's conversation about Tobias and the others being there in the gardens, and it pulled me out of my dream state. They wanted to turn me and use me for their own evil designs, but I was able to work my own magic on them. Before I could send word to you about their plan and that the others were in the gardens, I was fighting Tobias, and I didn't have time to call for help."

"You put Shelly and Michail into a nightmare first."

"Yes. I was so angry that they were traitors, that I did it to stop them from fighting any of us and also from communicating with their people. I was trying to do the same with Tobias while you were fighting him, but I was having trouble concentrating."

"Because you had been cut."

"In part, yes, but also because I kept thinking I might not be able to cut him again, and it would be better if I could distract him so you could get a killing blow in. I realized when I cut him, I didn't have the training or strength to really injure him badly."

"I was afraid he'd swing around and kill you."

"The thought had crossed my mind. I knew he was listening to my movements and my heart beating. I finally decided to really concentrate as hard as I could on my dream abilities like I had done with Shelly and Michail, and hoped if I could get him to raise his sword as if he were pointing to the greenhouse ceiling, you would have a chance to kill him. Except instead of you thrusting your sword at his heart right away, you were just staring at him as if you were shocked. I didn't want to say anything because I was afraid if I did, I would break my concentration, and I would lose control over him."

"But you didn't lose your concentration over Shelly or Michail."

"Right. But they might have been weaker vampires, which could possibly have made a difference. I tried to do the same thing with Regina when Jasmine was fighting her, and with Clarissa when Caitlin was dealing with her, but I couldn't seem to. Maybe because I was too worried about everyone being hurt."

"And because you had been hurt."

"That could be true."

He kissed her and hugged her close. "Don't go traveling as a vampire without me, next time."

She smiled and kissed him back. "Don't tell me you're going to start ordering me around because you turned me."

"I wouldn't dare, not knowing everything that you're now capable of doing. You can chase me in my dreams though, if you would like."

"I will do much more than that. I love you, you know," Fiona said, sighing against his chest.

He kissed the top of her head. "No more than I love you."

"Good. Then you don't mind if we redecorate this bedroom, do you? I want a blue comforter."

He chuckled. "I would do anything for you to make you happy, as happy as you make me just being with you."

"I'm glad I spilled sticky soda on you that day at the Dallas mall so long ago."

"I'm glad your dad was instrumental in getting us together both times."

"Me too."

Then they finally drifted off to sleep and this time Fiona let Arman chase her—but next time? Well, it was a toss-up. Adding some variety to life was what it was all about!

EPILOGUE

Despite Jasmine's sincerity in wanting Fiona to become a guild member and learn how to be an assassin with her, Fiona knew she was too newly turned. And she was still practicing her dreaming skills, and everyone loved how she could give them the most pleasant of dreams but still get enough sleep during the night. Besides, now that she had parents again, though she was eighteen, they wanted her to finish up her high school diploma online. So she was still working on it.

Her birthday party had been the best ever, with presents galore from family and friends, but more than anything, her birthday party had been the best because she had so many friends and she was able to reconnect with her family. Even the vampires who had fought off their enemies stayed to enjoy the party. It had really been great. And this time, she had danced with Arman during most of the songs—not having to stop because of fights between mummies and toga-dressed teens. She loved dancing with her father, and then her brother too.

She and Justin were thrilled to be getting to know her

parents, both of whom were working with hunters who had been newly turned to teach them their new vampire ways, including Fiona and Justin. They treated him like he had always been their son. They also treated the vampire princes and their mates as family. Of course everyone wanted to know what was taking Ruric so long to find a girlfriend. But he said the right girl for him was somewhere in a faraway galaxy, and Fiona wondered if he would ever truly find one.

Life with Arman had been great. Sure, he could be bossy at times, a little controlling, but mostly because he was concerned for her safety like Levka was with Caitlin. Stasio was with Jasmine also, but he was really low key about it because she had a reputation as a vampire assassin to maintain. Fiona was glad they had so many other vampires in the group who were the best of friends too. Her whole world had changed for the better once Arman had come to her rescue and she had reconnected with him and joined him in his world.

ARMAN WAS THRILLED to have Fiona in his life and he knew she felt the same about him, even when he was concerned for her safety and was a little bit overprotective. He loved how she infiltrated his dreams at night to make them even more pleasant and had become his vampire mate for all eternity. He couldn't have been happier than the way that things had turned out between the two of them.

He was glad he had accepted that he had needed his friends in the quest to keep her safe and that everyone loved her as much as he did. Some of that might have been because she chased all their nightmares away. Even Levka had privately told her he appreciated how she had helped Caitlin overcome her nightmares about the sharks in the ocean since she'd had two experiences of being in the water before she'd been rescued. Though he hadn't told Fiona how he was glad she'd helped deal with his nightmares, Arman knew he was glad for it.

Fiona had even given Ruric futuristic dreams that he had shared with them the next morning, just delighted. Whether any of that was anything more than fantastical dreams or maybe a hint of visions of the future, they didn't know, but Ruric loved it nonetheless.

Justin was busy with college schoolwork in Scotland, rather than returning to the States. In fact, everyone had stayed here. The estate was big enough for many more, and when Arman had a chance, he was taking Fiona and her family to see his Welsh castle.

Even Stasio's cousins and Jasmine's brother were hanging around for a bit. They said it was because they knew how Levka and his pack were always getting into trouble and it might behoove them to visit for a while longer. In truth? They loved the swimming pool and the tennis courts, the chef's outstanding meals, and the camaraderie they enjoyed at the estate for the time being. Arman and the others loved having them there.

He heard a splash in the pool and wondered who had gone swimming. Most everyone was just chilling in the living room except for Justin who was at a class at the college and Fiona who was finishing up a high school assignment on her computer in their bedroom, everything in their bedroom changed to blues. He loved it just as much as she did. Though if she had wanted an all-pink bedroom, he would have been just happy—as long as he had her in his life. He glanced out the window and saw her in the pool, fully dressed. She hadn't quite gotten her transporting skills down yet. Smiling, he headed into the swimming pool room, pulled off his shoes and jumped in, clothes and all.

She laughed. "You didn't have to join me out here wearing all your clothes."

"It's the easiest way I can take you back to our room." And then he transported them dripping wet there.

"I've got to work on transporting more."

"With me in tow."

"I have news," she said, wrapping her arms around him, pressing their wet bodies together.

"Oh?"

"I'm a high school graduate! Four months early. Now I can enroll in college. But I have to wait until the new session starts and I have to take the test, fill out the paperwork—"

"You're a vampire now."

She smiled brightly. "You're right. I can just"—she snapped her fingers—"transport into classes and finish up a degree in no time."

"Not transport."

"Hmm, I could convince the college to give me a degree."

He laughed. "You wouldn't learn anything that way. But we can certainly get you enrolled anywhere you want to go, no hassle at all."

"I want to go to college where my brother is attending."

"That's a given. And I'll go too."

"No way."

"Yep. Someone's got to watch out for you and your brother."

"Yeah, but my brother hasn't needed anyone watching out for him until I said I would go to college."

Arman smiled. "I've been here with you, but what do you think the others have been doing while he's in school?"

"Really?" She smiled. "You all are the best."

"I love you." He gave her a searing kiss, slipped his tongue into her mouth, and felt her growing canines.

"I'm working on that."

"It's only natural that they should extend when we're kissing." And he kissed her again.

She whispered, "I love you."

He was so glad she was one of them—fitting right in with her family and her vampire friends. It couldn't have been more perfect.

ACKNOWLEDGMENTS

Thanks so much to Donna Fourier and Darla Taylor for beta reading for me! You all are such a help! Thanks for everything.

ABOUT THE AUTHOR

Bestselling and award-winning author Terry Spear has written over eighty paranormal romance novels and four medieval Highland historical romances. Her first werewolf romance, *Heart of the Wolf*, was named a 2008 *Publishers Weekly*'s Best Book of the Year, and her subsequent titles have garnered high praise and hit the *USA Today* bestseller list. A retired officer of the U.S. Army Reserves, Terry lives in Spring, Texas, where she is working on her next wolf, jaguar, cougar, and bear shifter romances, continuing with her Highland medieval romances, and having fun with her young adult novels. When she's not writing, she's photographing everything that catches her eye, making teddy bears, and playing with her Havanese puppies and grandchildren. For more information, please visit www.terryspear.com, or follow her on Twitter, @TerrySpear. She is also on Facebook at http://www.facebook.com/terry.spear.

And on Wordpress at: Terry Spear's Shifters http://terryspear.wordpress.com/

ALSO BY TERRY SPEAR

Adult Titles

Romantic Suspense: Deadly Fortunes, In the Dead of the Night, Relative Danger, Bound by Danger

***

The Highlanders Series: His Wild Highland Lass (novella), Vexing the Highlander (novella), Winning the Highlander's Heart, The Accidental Highland Hero, Highland Rake, Taming the Wild Highlander, The Highlander, Her Highland Hero, The Viking's Highland Lass, My Highlander

Other historical romances: Lady Caroline & the Egotistical Earl, A Ghost of a Chance at Love

***

Heart of the Wolf Series: Heart of the Wolf, Destiny of the Wolf, To Tempt the Wolf, Legend of the White Wolf, Seduced by the Wolf, Wolf Fever, Heart of the Highland Wolf, Dreaming of the Wolf, A SEAL in Wolf's Clothing, A Howl for a Highlander, A Highland Werewolf Wedding, A SEAL Wolf Christmas, Silence of the Wolf, Hero of a Highland Wolf, A Highland Wolf Christmas; SEAL Wolf Hunting; A Silver Wolf Christmas, SEAL Wolf in Too Deep, Alpha Wolf Need Not Apply, Between a Wolf and a Hard Place, SEAL Wolf Undercover, Dreaming of a White Wolf Christmas, Flight of the White Wolf, All's Fair in Love and Wolf, A Billionaire Wolf for Christmas, SEAL Wolf Surrender, Silver Town Wolf: Home for the Holidays, Night of the Billionaire Wolf, You Had Me at Wolf, Joy to the Wolves, The Wolf Wore Plaid, Jingle Bell Wolf, The Best of Both Wolves, While the Wolf's

Away, Christmas Wolf Surprise, Wolf Takes the Lead, Wolf on the Wild Side, Her Wolf for the Holidays, A Good Wolf is Hard to Find (2024), Mated for Christmas (2024)

SEAL Wolves: To Tempt the Wolf, A SEAL in Wolf's Clothing, A SEAL Wolf Christmas; SEAL Wolf Hunting, A SEAL Wolf in Too Deep, SEAL Wolf Undercover, SEAL Wolf Surrender

Silver Town Wolves: Destiny of the Wolf, Wolf Fever, Dreaming of the Wolf, Silence of the Wolf; A Silver Wolf Christmas, Between a Wolf and a Hard Place, Home for the Holidays, Jingle Bell Wolf

Wolff Family Lodge Wolves: You Had Me at Wolf, Wolf on the Wild Side, A Good Wolf is Hard to Find

Highland Wolves: Heart of the Highland Wolf, A Howl for a Highlander, A Highland Werewolf Wedding, Hero of a Highland Wolf, A Highland Wolf Christmas, The Wolf Wore Plaid, Her Wolf for the Holidays

Billionaire Wolf Series: A Billionaire in Wolf's Clothing, A Billionaire Wolf for Christmas, Night of the Billionaire Wolf, Wolf Takes the Lead

White Wolf Series: Legend of the White Wolf, Dreaming of a White Wolf Christmas, Flight of the White Wolf, While the Wolf's Away, Mated for Christmas

Red Wolf Series: Seduced by the Wolf, Joy to the Wolves, The Best of Both Wolves, Christmas Wolf Surprise

Wolf Novellas: Day of the Wolf, Seal Wolf Pursuit, Wolf to the Rescue, Night of the Wolf, United Shifter Force

***

Heart of the Jaguar Series: Savage Hunger, Jaguar Fever, Jaguar Hunt, Jaguar Pride, A Very Jaguar Christmas, You Had Me at Jaguar, The Witch and the Jaguar, Dawn of the Jaguar

***

Heart of the Cougar Series: Cougar's Mate, Call of the Cougar, Taming the Wild Cougar, Covert Cougar Christmas, a novella, Double Cougar Trouble, Cougar Undercover, Cougar Magic, Cougar Halloween Mischief, Falling for the Cougar, Cougar Christmas Calamity, Catch the Cougar (Halloween Novella), You Had Me at Cougar, Saving the White Cougar, Big Cat Magic

***

White Bear Series: Loving the White Bear, Claiming the White Bear, Bear of a Halloween

Grizzly Bear Series: Bear in Mind

***

Wolves of Old: Wolf Pack

Vampire romances: Killing the Bloodlust, Deadly Liaisons, Huntress for Hire, Forbidden Love, Deadly Liaisons, Vampire Redemption, Primal Desire

Vampire Novellas: The Siren's Lure, Vampiric Calling, Seducing the Huntress

***

Comedy Romance: Exchanging Grooms, Marriage, Las Vegas Style

***

Science Fiction: Galaxy Warrior

Young Adult Titles

The World of Fae:

The Dark Fae

The Deadly Fae

The Winged Fae

The Ancient Fae

Dragon Fae

Hawk Fae

Phantom Fae

Golden Fae

Falcon Fae

Woodland Fae

Angel Fae

***

The World of Elf:

The Shadow Elf

The Darkland Elf

Warrior Elf

***

Blood Moon Series:

Kiss of the VampireMy Book

Bite of the Vampire

The Vampire Chronicles Series:

The Vampire in My Dreams

Demon Guardian Series:

The Trouble with Demons

Demon Trouble, Too

Demon Hunter

Non-Series for Now:
Ghostly Liaisons
The Beast Within
Courtly Masquerade
Deidre's Secret

The Magic of Inherian:
The Scepter of Salvation
The Mage of Monrovia
Emerald Isle of Mists

Made in the USA
Middletown, DE
20 January 2024